Praise for
Junk

"Forget about all the TV pundits and op-ed columnists droning on about America's problems. Playwright Ayad Akhtar is the diagnostician the nation needs to interpret its faltering health....In *Junk*, his thrilling new play...Akhtar takes on the equally explosive subjects of modern finance and the new religion of money. And once again he provides an unflinchingly candid cross section of attitudes and positions in which our sympathies and antipathies keep shifting along lines that are too complex to be straightforwardly ideological.... What's most impressive about *Junk* is the brilliant way Akhtar crunches the social, political, and economic data of this greedy new world, a precursor to the way we live today."

—Charles McNulty, *Los Angeles Times*

"Whip-smart....An intimate, accessible tale on an epic canvas.... Akhtar writes crackling, rapid-fire, overlapping dialogue like David Mamet, but it's infused with Shakespearean scope and pop-culture references. There are nods to the Bard's *Merchant of Venice, Julius Caesar,* and history plays, lines from the Bible, and the 1987 film *Wall Street* and the freewheeling exuberance of *The Wolf of Wall Street*." —Pam Kragen, *San Diego Union-Tribune*

"A massively ambitious play. It succeeds magnificently on many levels, and it should head to Broadway, where it will be not only close to Wall Street, but even more accessible to those many in the public with a growing fascination in finance, economics, and social policy." —Brad Auerbach, *Forbes*

"*Junk* unfolds like a big, blockbuster novel—lots of twists and turns, and goods and evils (okay, mostly evils). It's an epic seduction, in fact, that involves everyone in the piece. At the same time, the playwright underpins the antics with serious themes and key questions." —Jeff Smith, *San Diego Reader*

Praise for

The Invisible Hand

"With *The Invisible Hand,* Ayad Akhtar solidifies the reputation he forged with *Disgraced* as a first-rate writer of fierce, well-crafted dramas that employ topicality but are not limited by it....The prime theme is pulsing and alive: when human lives become just one more commodity to be traded, blood eventually flows in the streets."
— Brendan Lemon, *Financial Times*

"Raises probing questions about the roots of the Islamic terrorism that has rattled the world for the last decade and more."
— Charles Isherwood, *New York Times*

"A hand-wringing, throat-clenching thriller...that grabs you and won't let go." — Jesse Green, *New York Magazine*

"Confirms the Pakistani-American playwright as one of the theater's most original, exciting new voices....In this tight, plot-driven thriller, Akhtar again turns hypersensitive subjects into thought-provoking and thoughtful drama. But here he also brings a grasp of money—big money—not to mention the market's unsettling connections to international politics." — Linda Winer, *Newsday*

"Politically provocative....A scary (and dreadfully funny) treatise on the universality of human greed." — Marilyn Stasio, *Variety*

"A tragically contemporary thriller....There has been precious little activity on this front since Jerry Sterner's *Other People's Money* and Caryl Churchill's *Serious Money*....Mr. Akhtar makes up for this oversight with a vengeance." — Harry Haun, *New York Observer*

Praise for

The Who & The What

"Disarmingly funny. A fiery...probing new play, crackling with ideas." —Charles Isherwood, *New York Times*

"At its fiercest, *The Who & The What* bares some of the same teeth as Akhtar's riveting 2013 Pulitzer-copping *Disgraced*....Akhtar's who and what are potent." —Bob Verini, *Variety*

"Vibrant. Strong and colorful. A culture-clash drama simmering with humor." —Associated Press

"A heady exploration of how one's hoped-for path in life can crash against the ramparts of family and society....*The Who & The What* helps lift a veil on a spiritual tradition that's little-portrayed on American stages. The 'what' of this ambitious play could just about fill a book by itself; the 'who' at its heart is one lively, vibrant, and questioning voice." —James Hebert, *San Diego Union-Tribune*

"Fearless...powerful...Ayad Akhtar is...prodigiously talented." —Jeremy Gerard, *Deadline*

"Continually absorbing...Akhtar has a splendid command of structure and...a fine ear for dialogue." —*The New Yorker*

"Akhtar is a provocative, wise, and funny playwright." —Steve Suskin, *Huffington Post*

"Crackles with intelligence and behavioral truth....Akhtar is so eminently gifted in writing scenes that quake with powerful emotion." —Charles McNulty, *Los Angeles Times*

Praise for

Disgraced

"The best play I saw last year.... A quick-witted and shattering drama.... *Disgraced* rubs all kinds of unexpected raw spots with intelligence and humor." —Linda Winer, *Newsday*

"A sparkling and combustible contemporary drama.... Ayad Akhtar's one-act play deftly mixes the political and personal, exploring race, freedom of speech, political correctness, even the essence of Islam and Judaism. The insidery references to the Hamptons and Bucks County, Pennsylvania, and art critic Jerry Saltz are just enough to make audience members feel smart.... Akhtar...has lots to say about America and the world today. He says it all compellingly, and none of it is comforting." —Philip Boroff, *Bloomberg Businessweek*

"Compelling.... *Disgraced* raises and toys with provocative and nuanced ideas." —Jesse Oxfeld, *New York Observer*

"A continuously engaging, vitally engaged play about thorny questions of identity and religion in the contemporary world.... In dialogue that bristles with wit and intelligence, Mr. Akhtar...puts contemporary attitudes toward religion under a microscope, revealing how tenuous self-image can be for people born into one way of being who have embraced another.... Everyone has been told that politics and religion are two subjects that should be off-limits at social gatherings. But watching Mr. Akhtar's characters rip into these forbidden topics, there's no arguing that they make for ear-tickling good theater." —Charles Isherwood, *New York Times*

"A blistering social drama about the racial prejudices that secretly persist in progressive cultural circles." —Marilyn Stasio, *Variety*

"Terrific....*Disgraced*...unfolds with speed, energy, and crackling wit....The evening will come to a shocking end, but before that, there is the sparkling conversation, expertly rendered on the page by Akhtar....Talk of 9/11, of Israel and Iran, of terrorism and airport security, all evokes uncomfortable truths. Add a liberal flow of alcohol and a couple of major secrets suddenly revealed, and you've got yourself one dangerous dinner party....In the end, one can debate what the message of the play really is. Is it that we cannot escape our roots, or perhaps simply that we don't ever really know who we are, deep down, until something forces us to confront it? Whatever it is, when you finally hear the word 'disgraced' in the words of one of these characters, you will no doubt feel a chill down your spine."
—Jocelyn Noveck, Associated Press

"Offers an engaging snapshot of the challenge for upwardly mobile Islamic Americans in the post-9/11 age."
—Thom Geier, *Entertainment Weekly*

"*Disgraced* stands among recent marks of an increasing and welcome phenomenon: the arrival of South Asian and Middle Eastern Americans as presences in our theater's dramatis personae, matching their presence in our daily life. Like all such phenomena, it carries a double significance. An achievement and a sign of recognition for those it represents, for the rest of us it constitutes the theatrical equivalent of getting to know the new neighbors—something we had better do if we plan to survive as a civil society."
—Michael Feingold, *Village Voice*

"Ninety minutes of sharp contemporary theatre at its argumentative, and disturbing, best."   —Robert McCrum, *The Guardian*

Junk

ALSO BY AYAD AKHTAR

The Invisible Hand
The Who & The What
Disgraced
American Dervish

Junk

A PLAY

AYAD AKHTAR

BACK BAY BOOKS
Little, Brown and Company
New York Boston London

Back Bay Books / Little, Brown and Company
Hachette Book Group
1290 Avenue of the Americas, New York, NY 10104
littlebrown.com

First edition: November 2017

Back Bay Books is an imprint of Little, Brown and Company, a division of Hachette Book Group, Inc. The Back Bay Books name and logo are trademarks of Hachette Book Group, Inc.

The publisher is not responsible for websites (or their content) that are not owned by the publisher.

The Hachette Speakers Bureau provides a wide range of authors for speaking events. To find out more, go to hachettespeakersbureau.com or call (866) 376-6591.

ISBN 978-0-316-55072-7
LCCN 2017942050

10 9 8 7 6 5 4 3 2

LSC-C

Printed in the United States of America

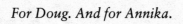

For Doug. And for Annika.

THE POETICS OF MONEY

History does not repeat itself, but it does rhyme.

—Often attributed to Mark Twain

Whoever said it, said it well, but perhaps not forcefully enough. For to speak of history's rhyming schemes is already to imply—without insisting—that our tribes, our nations, their defining quandaries and quiddities, are substantially the result of poetic concoction. Stories, really. For history's animating spirits are never driven by mere actualities; but rather shaped by locution, directed by metaphor, nourished by meaning. Poetic compression and narrative contest (and the resulting triumphs or defeats)—these are history's architectural fundaments. These are what we see as the ever-molting, ever-recurring patterns recognizable in history's rhymes, whether eye or end, rich or slant.

To some, Shakespeare virtually forged Englishness in the crucible of his nine Elizabethan English-history plays. But he did so with little fidelity to the merely actual. For whatever else *Henry V* is—a critique of canny power; a celebration of compassionate kingship; a demonstration of England's innate superiority over its French neighbor—it is certainly not anything like what truly happened. But we don't care. For we recall a diplomatic insult in a crate of tennis balls, a blood-warming paean to noble death on St. Crispin's day, a climactic wooing that seduces even the most cynical of us into believing that peace can always be made with our enemy. By means of elision and elaboration, personification, emotional investment in point of view, the play brings us to the recognition that history is made of us, that we can see and know it because we can see and know ourselves in it.

*　　*　　*

Those familiar with the financial history of the 1980s will seek and find correspondences in *Junk* with the *merely actual* events of that era. Indeed, one need not have gone to business school to have at least a cursory familiarity with the Revlon and RJR-Nabisco deals, the techniques of the rising titans who engineered them, and the resulting cautionary tales that landed more than a few of that vanguard generation in prison. To those looking, the correspondences will abound, but they are not primary.

They are, in fact, misleading.

At the center of this story is Robert Merkin, a remarkable man who raises money by selling debt. His means, his ends—creative, disruptive, profoundly individualist—are having an outsized, even unprecedented effect on American life. But in assessing Merkin, in taking stock of his optimizing, morally driven commitment to capitalism, we could make the mistake of believing that Merkin's historical corollaries might point the way to the play's secret meaning. Not so. For Merkin has been fashioned from the jetsam of the past to speak to us of who we are now. What our near-religious commitment to capital growth has brought us to, now. What world we have brought into being under this regime of finance. Now.

It is easy to criticize capitalism, and even easier to enjoy its benefits. And neither drama nor the world at large needs another screed decrying the predations of greed. What I did believe—and my partner in this process, Doug Hughes, believed as well—was that emotional understanding and dramatic engagement (the stuff of poetry, if you will) must come before all judgment. So we strove to make of this the best tale we could, one with the breadth of our shared ambition to convey not only contemporary finance's mythic reach, but also its historical roots. For indeed, no aspect of our collective life today is untouched by the poetics of money forged in the crucible of that storied era.

Ayad Akhtar
Peterborough, New Hampshire
May 2017

PRODUCTION HISTORY

Junk had its world premiere on August 5, 2016, at La Jolla Playhouse, California (Christopher Ashley, artistic director; Michael S. Rosenberg, managing director). It was directed by Doug Hughes; the set design was by John Lee Beatty; the costume design was by William Mellette; the lighting design was by Ben Stanton; the sound design was by Mark Bennett; and the stage manager was Charles Means. The cast was as follows:

Judy Chen	Jennifer Ikeda
Robert Merkin	Josh Cooke
Raúl Rivera	Armando Riesco
Murray Lefkowitz / Chen's Lawyer	Jason Kravits
Israel Peterman	Matthew Rauch
Charlene Stewart	Zora Howard
Thomas Everson	Linus Roache
Maximilien Cizik	Henry Stram
Jacqueline Blount	Zakiya Iman Markland
Leo Tresler	David Rasche
Boris Pronsky	Jeff Marlow
Mark O'Hare / Merkin's Lawyer / Union Worker	Sean McIntyre

Devon Atkins / Waiter ....Hunter Spangler
Amy Merkin ....Annika Boras
Giuseppi Addesso............................... Benjamin Burdick
Kevin Walsh.. Keith Wallace
Corrigan Wiley / Union Rep / Curt.......................... Tony Carlin

Junk

We would rather be ruined than changed...
—W. H. Auden

MAJOR CHARACTERS

THE RAIDERS:

ROBERT MERKIN—Early 40s. "Bob." Junk Bond Trader
   at Sacker-Lowell, an investment bank. Merkin is an
   unusual combination of charismatic leader and behind-
   the-desk functionary. On the strength of unparalleled
   focus and remarkable intellectual gifts, he has emerged
   as the financier of the age.

RAÚL RIVERA—Mid-30s. Lawyer for Sacker-Lowell. Of
   Cuban extraction. Wry, playful, ruthless.

ISRAEL PETERMAN—Late 30s. "Izzy." A corporate
   raider. Sacramento-born. Intense, rough-hewn,
   tenacious. Eager to propel himself—by whatever means
   necessary—to the front ranks of American business.

BORIS PRONSKY—Late 40s. An arbitrageur. Makes
   money off rumor and intrigue. All facade, no substance.
   The proverbial little man in a big man's body.

MANAGEMENT AND ITS ALLIES:

THOMAS EVERSON, JR.—50s. "Tom." Chief Executive
   of Everson Steel and United, the erstwhile manufacturing
   behemoth and still-member of the Dow Industrial

Average. The steel business has fallen on hard times, and Everson Jr. continues to see through the diversification of the company begun under his father's regime. Though not quite the brilliant businessman his father was, Everson Jr. makes up for it with heart and in loyalty.

MAXIMILIEN CIZIK—Late 40s. "Max." Investment Banker at Lausanne & Co. Adviser to Everson. Urbane, measured, sophisticated. Born in Prague, but brought up in America. Lausanne & Co. is a leading advisory investment bank, and one of the last of such still connected to the great nineteenth-century European merchant banks.

JACQUELINE BLOUNT—Late 20s. "Jackie." Lawyer for Lausanne & Co. African-American. Harvard Law. Harvard Business. Appealing, ambitious. With balls and charm to boot.

LEO TRESLER—Mid-50s. A private equity magnate. Passionate, pompous, lovable, and very rich. A lion of a man with something of a Texas swagger, despite being born and raised in Connecticut.

LAW ENFORCEMENT:

GIUSEPPE ADDESSO—Mid-40s. "Joe." US Attorney of New York, Southern District. Italian-American. Ambitious.

KEVIN WALSH—Early 30s. Assistant US Attorney, Fraud Unit. African-American. Punctilious and indefatigable.

OTHER:

JUDY CHEN—Early 30s. A writer. Third-generation Chinese-American. Thoughtful, penetrating, and undaunted by the titans about whom she is writing.

AMY MERKIN—40s. Robert's wife, his business school sweetheart. A financial wizard in her own right. Merkin's deepest collaborator.

SUPPORTING AND MINOR CHARACTERS

(Can be doubled as fitting)

MARK O'HARE—40s. An arbitrageur. Irish-American. Born and raised in the heyday of Hell's Kitchen. A street fighter who rides the market's currents.

CORRIGAN WILEY—50s. Attorney for O'Hare. Gruff and loyal. Hailing from a family that has served as counsel to generations of the Irish Mob.

DEVON ATKINS—Late 20s. An arbitrageur. A kid. In over his head.

MURRAY LEFKOWITZ—Late 40s. One of Merkin's investors.

CHARLENE STEWART—20s. Assistant to Robert Merkin.

LAWYERS AND OTHERS: As needed.

A NOTE ON SETTING

Great lengths should not be taken to bring the various scene settings too realistically into being, for the events that unfold in what follows are conceived to take place on the stage of what we could call our collective memory. Put into other words, the play is a ritual enactment of an origin myth.

The premium must be on establishing and maintaining an unbroken, vital flow, with a fluidity evocative of the movement of the mind. Allegro con brio, if you will.

The insinuation of the mid-1980s in costume and design must not be overdone. The world evoked in the events depicted—the origins of debt financing—are not just a matter of the past, but represent an ethos and an ontology very much central to what we call the world today.

Act One

JUDY CHEN.

Quicksilver smarts, striking beauty. Alone on stage as she addresses the audience.

CHEN: This is a story of kings—or what passes for kings these days. Kings then, bedecked in Brooks Brothers and Brioni, enthroned in sky-high castles on opposing coasts, embroiled in a battle over, well, what else, money. *(Beat)* When did money become the thing? I mean the *only* thing? Upgrade your place in line, or your prison cell, for a fee. Rent out your womb to carry someone else's child. Buy a stranger's life insurance policy—pay the premium until they die—then collect the benefit. Oh, and cash. Whose idea was it to start charging us just to get cash?

—LIGHTS UP ON:

ROBERT MERKIN.

CHEN (CONT'D): The mid-eighties. 1985 to be exact. I'd been writing for *Forbes*, the *Wall Street Journal*. And yes, I was used to being surrounded by talk of money. But '85 was when I started to sense something new. A pluck and pugnacity, a frenzied zeal in people's eyes. It was like a new religion was being born...

LOS ANGELES. SACKER-LOWELL & ASSOCIATES.

Robert Merkin, Israel Peterman, Raúl Rivera. In the middle of a strategy session.

MERKIN: Izzy, Izzy, no. Don't use that word—

PETERMAN: Which one?

MERKIN: *Limit.* Not when you're talking about what's *yours*...

PETERMAN: Even if I want to impose cuts—

MERKIN: That's another. *Impose.*

RIVERA: *Reform* is better.

MERKIN: You are going to bring *reform*...

RIVERA: You have a *vision*.

MERKIN: Which is why you're buying the company. To help Everson Steel *grow*.

RIVERA: *Change. Transform.*

MERKIN: Human beings are creatures of hope. When you talk about yourself, your company, always use words cut from the cloth of hope.

PETERMAN: Cut from the cloth of hope. Fuck me.

RIVERA: It's good, huh?

MERKIN: But when you talk about *them*...

PETERMAN: Tom Everson?

MERKIN: Current owners. Current management. *That's* when you use words like *limit*.

RIVERA: *They* are *limited*.

MERKIN: They don't get with the program? They're headed for crisis. Collapse.

RIVERA: Catastrophe.

MERKIN: Even better. But *you*. Your company...

RIVERA *(Selling it)*: Saratoga-McDaniels...

PETERMAN: Has a *vision* for *reform*.

RIVERA: That's good.

MERKIN: Right. It's the things people don't realize they're hearing...

RIVERA: The echoes, the hidden logic.

MERKIN: The hidden logic. That's what sinks in. Makes people not just think, but *feel*. That's the way to their hearts.

PETERMAN: Is there a list or something?

MERKIN: List?

PETERMAN: Of words I should use, not use?

Merkin and Rivera share a look.

RIVERA: I mean...—why not? We'll make a list.

MERKIN: Great.

Rivera takes up a legal pad. Starts jotting. Just as...

CHARLENE, Merkin's assistant, appears—

CHARLENE: Mr. Merkin, Murray Lefkowitz on the line.

MERKIN: Thanks, Charlene. *(To Peterman, Rivera)* Let me get this.

Merkin steps into—

—A POOL OF LIGHT.

—ANOTHER POOL APPEARS, SHOWING:

MURRAY.

A schlemiel. The conversation is quick, percussive.

MERKIN: What do you want, Murray?

MURRAY *(Beat)*: I know. I should have—

MERKIN: I gave up on you, Murr.

MURRAY: I'm sorry, Bob.

MERKIN: Did I do something? Did I say something—

MURRAY: Of course not.

MERKIN: So what is it? You can't call me back? It's crunch time for this new bond issue. You know that—

MURRAY: I know.

MERKIN: Okay, well…Anyway, we're selling junk in Izzy Peterman's company. Saratoga-McDaniels. For him to go after Everson Steel. The bonds are paying seventeen percent, quarterly coupon. Rated triple C like usual—

MURRAY: Bob—

MERKIN *(Over)*: Murr, I want you to come in for more than usual. We're making our first play on the Dow—

MURRAY: Right—

MERKIN: Shoulder to shoulder, Murray. Deal by deal. That's what we've been doing. Making 'em see we can be the big *machers,* too.

MURRAY: I, uh…

MERKIN: I need you. More than ever.

MURRAY: Bob. I have to talk to you.

MERKIN: So talk.

MURRAY: It's Macie.

MERKIN *(Sudden shift)*: Is she okay? Is your wife okay?

MURRAY: No, she's fine. It's just—she has a friend.

MERKIN: A friend—

MURRAY: Who's married to Greenfield.

Beat.

MERKIN: Murray.

MURRAY: He went belly up, Bob. Bought a ton of junk from First City—

MERKIN: Greenfield's a cheat. He was buying from First City because I won't sell to him anymore.

MURRAY: I know—

MERKIN: Do you?

MURRAY: I don't like him any better than you do.

MERKIN: Let me get this straight. First City's peddling shit and calling it junk and you stop returning my phone calls?

MURRAY: That's not it. Macie just—I mean—I'm at a hundred million in liquid assets. Bob, she just—she doesn't want me—to take any more risks. She wants me to stop.

MERKIN: She? Or you?

MURRAY: I don't want you to be mad.

MERKIN: Four, maybe five million? That's what you came to me with seven years ago.

MURRAY: It was Macie's money.

MERKIN: No.

MURRAY: It was all hers. Her dad's.

MERKIN: *That* was hers. The rest? *I* made you. I make you rich, you and Macie, then she hears about First City selling crap to that moron Greenfield and you stop returning my calls?

MURRAY: I was afraid.

MERKIN: Of what, Murray? Of what? Making money?

Beat.

MURRAY: She doesn't like that people call it junk, Bob. She

doesn't like me putting all that money in something that people talk about like it's garbage—

MERKIN: It's a misnomer, Murr. You know that, right?

MURRAY: But—

MERKIN *(Continuing)*: If I got you into bonds in IBM or GE, Macie wouldn't have a problem with that...

MURRAY: Probably not.

MERKIN: Because she's heard of those companies. Everybody has. But the returns on those bonds aren't anywhere near as good as what I sell you. I am selling you into the future. That's what you have to tell her. Izzy Peterman? Saratoga-McDaniels? Tomorrow's Jack Welch, tomorrow's General Electric.

MURRAY: Bob...

MERKIN: Listen to me, Murr. We've known each other a long time.

MURRAY: I know.

MERKIN: We've come a long way. Since you sold me that T-shirt on Canal Street.

MURRAY: I remember.

MERKIN: Right. So this is what I'm going to do. You come in on this deal now, I will buy you out if you want out.

MURRAY: You will?

MERKIN: I promise. You want out early? Just say the word.

MURRAY: You'd do that for me?

MERKIN: I promise.

—LIGHTS OUT ON MERKIN AND MURRAY.

BACK AT THE CONFERENCE TABLE.

Peterman makes notes as Rivera speaks:

RIVERA: Change, choice, choose... Pursue—

PETERMAN: Lead. How about that?

RIVERA: That's great.

PETERMAN: I am leading a vision—

RIVERA: *We* is better than *I*.

PETERMAN: We are leading a vision...

RIVERA: It's always we when you're talking about yourself, your company.... We, our, us...

PETERMAN: Right.

RIVERA: —but when you talk about Everson, their CEO, management? *Them. They.*

PETERMAN: They're *limited*. They're headed for *crisis*.

RIVERA: Which is just the truth.

PETERMAN: Well, like my dad always says, it's easier to sell something when you believe it.

RIVERA: And nothing easier to believe than the truth.

PETERMAN: *We* are leading a *vision* of *courage*.

RIVERA: Mmm. A *path* of courage. A vision of...

PETERMAN: Choice?

RIVERA *(With a shrug)*: You'll get the hang of it.

Merkin enters. Energized.

MERKIN: Murray's in for fifty.

RIVERA: Wait. Murray's in for—?

MERKIN: Fifty million.

RIVERA: How?

MERKIN: If he wants out, I buy him out.

RIVERA: I mean...

MERKIN: He won't want out...

RIVERA: With him in, that puts us over five hundred.

MERKIN: By this time tomorrow? Seven.

PETERMAN: Seven hundred million?

MERKIN: Yep.

PETERMAN: I still don't get it.

MERKIN: Get what?

PETERMAN: How you raise that kind of money. My company's not even worth half of that.

RIVERA: The Merkin magic.

PETERMAN: No, seriously. What are you telling people that makes them want to give you seven hundred million dollars to give me?

MERKIN: The truth. This is the deal of the decade.

RIVERA: Get in now on the deal that changes all the rules.

PETERMAN: *This* deal? — *That's* what you've been saying?

MERKIN: Yes.

PETERMAN: So you've been *mentioning* Veronica...

MERKIN: What's Veronica?

RIVERA *(To Merkin)*: Their code name for Everson Steel.

PETERMAN *(Abrupt, to Rivera)*: —you've been mentioning Veronica *by name?*

RIVERA: People want to know what the money's for.

PETERMAN: *In writing?*

MERKIN: What's the problem?

Peterman gets up. Troubled.

PETERMAN: Bob...Before you came along, nobody did deals like this. I mean, to some of these blue bloods, these aren't even deals. *Takeover* is like a fucking four-letter word to them.

RIVERA: They're living in the middle ages. So that's our problem?

PETERMAN: My point is this is the first play you're making on a Dow Jones Industrial.

MERKIN: And?

PETERMAN: That's their holy of holies, Bob. They don't want you inside that.

MERKIN: It's a free country, Izzy.

PETERMAN: Whatever it is, everyone and their proctologist'll be crawling up the ass of this deal to see what stinks.

RIVERA: And you're worried about *what* exactly?

PETERMAN: Paperwork you filed for this raise said the money's for a *blind pool*...

RIVERA: So?

PETERMAN: *Blind* means I'm not supposed to know what the money's for. Not yet. If I do, and I don't say, that's a *disclosure violation*.

RIVERA: You disclose now? You kiss this deal good-bye.

PETERMAN: I don't know that? Why the fuck do you think I've been calling it *Veronica?*

MERKIN: What's that from anyway?

RIVERA: Tom Everson's dad. Dated Veronica Lake.

MERKIN: The actress?

PETERMAN: Back in the day. So the rumor goes.

RIVERA: I'm the lawyer. Let me be the lawyer.

MERKIN: Raúl's right. Leave the legalities to him.

Merkin's assistant, Charlene, appears again.

CHARLENE: Making a lunch run.

MERKIN *(To Peterman)*: What do you want?

PETERMAN: What's the place?

CHARLENE: It's a Jewish deli.

PETERMAN: Get me a matzo brei.

MERKIN: You want matzo brei?

PETERMAN: If they have it.

MERKIN: They don't have it.

PETERMAN: It's a Jewish deli. *(To Charlene)* Just ask.

MERKIN: This is Beverly Hills. They don't have matzo brei.

RIVERA: What's matzo brei?

MERKIN: Eggs and matzo. Like a matzo omelet. Disgusting.

PETERMAN *(To Merkin)*: What are you having?

RIVERA: The man hasn't had anything but ham and pickles on a toasted roll for…what—ten years?

MERKIN: And lemonade.

PETERMAN: Ham?

MERKIN: What?

PETERMAN: Really, Bob?

MERKIN: What are you, my rabbi?

PETERMAN: I thought it was a Jewish deli?

MERKIN: It's Beverly Hills.

RIVERA: Get me a Reuben.

PETERMAN: A Reuben? Who's the Jew? Who's the Cuban? *(To Charlene)* If they don't have matzo brei, get me like him. Hold the cheese. And a Diet Pepsi. Not Coke. Pepsi.

As Charlene exits, Peterman continues:

PETERMAN (CONT'D): So at forty-two and a half a share, seven hundred million gets me to thirty-five percent. What's the plan for the rest?

MERKIN: Amy and I went through Everson's numbers last night.

RIVERA: His wife is a genius with spreadsheets.

PETERMAN: Wait—you guys got Everson numbers?

RIVERA: Detailed statements. Line items from every division.

PETERMAN: You got inside numbers? How?

RIVERA: Someone I know.

PETERMAN: From where?

RIVERA: What do you care?

MERKIN *(Picking up)*: Anyway, it turns out the pharmaceutical divisions they bought ten years ago are throwing off serious cash.

PETERMAN: Okay...

MERKIN: That cash flow can be used as collateral.

PETERMAN: Collateral.

RIVERA: On a loan. For the rest of the money.

PETERMAN: We're going to take out a *loan* against Everson Steel?

MERKIN: Yes.

PETERMAN: But I don't own it yet.

MERKIN: Doesn't matter.

PETERMAN: Who came up with this?

MERKIN: I did.

PETERMAN: You came up with this?

RIVERA: They didn't just put him on the cover of *Time* magazine for nothing.

MERKIN: I didn't want to be on the cover of *Time* magazine.

RIVERA: You came off great.

MERKIN: They called me a job killer.

RIVERA: They also called you *America's Alchemist*. Turning debt into cash. From nothing, something.

MERKIN *(Ignoring)*: I'm not killing jobs. I'm *creating* them. They're always looking for the simple story. The good guy, the bad guy. They don't do their homework. They don't understand how the real world works.

RIVERA: I know, Bob. I know...

MERKIN: And that stupid story about the mining helmet again. I never wore a mining helmet to work.

PETERMAN: Mining helmet?

Pause.

MERKIN: You didn't read the article?

PETERMAN: Not yet, Bob. Sorry.

RIVERA: First couple of years out of school, he and Amy were living in her parents' basement out in Trenton—

MERKIN: I was taking the bus into the city five thirty every morning. Two hours wasted. So I worked. But it was usually pretty dark. So I'd work by flashlight. Somehow that becomes me wearing a mining helmet?

PETERMAN: I say fuck 'em. Fuck 'em where they live.

RIVERA: What does that even mean?

PETERMAN: It means, when we win? When I own Everson Steel? I'm changing the name.

—IMMEDIATE SHIFT TO:

NEW YORK. EVERSON STEEL HEADQUARTERS.

Tom Everson. Max Cizik. Jacqueline Blount.

Management, investment banking advising, and legal, respectively. Gathered for a strategy meeting at the headquarters of one of America's bellwether companies.

Everson in a summer seersucker. Cizik and Blount in suits.

EVERSON: A takeover.

CIZIK: Yes, Tom.

EVERSON: Takeover.

CIZIK: Yes. Tom.

EVERSON: My company? Everson Steel?

CIZIK: That's what other clients are telling us—It's what they're hearing on the street.

EVERSON: What's this guy's name again?

BLOUNT: Peterman. Israel Peterman.

EVERSON: *Israel.*

CIZIK: Goes by "Izzy."

BLOUNT: He's from Sacramento. Owns a drugstore chain.

CIZIK: Father owns a clothing company. Smart guy. Likeable.

EVERSON: What are they, Jewish Rockefellers?

CIZIK: Hardly.

BLOUNT: Other holdings include bowling equipment...

EVERSON: Bowling equipment?

BLOUNT: Hi-fi stereos, shopping malls—

EVERSON: Where exactly is the money for this coming from?

CIZIK: Robert Merkin. Sacker-Lowell.

BLOUNT: Junk bonds.

CIZIK: And creative financing. Merkin's done this thing in the past. He uses a takeover target's own cash flow as *collateral.*

EVERSON: Collateral?

CIZIK: On a loan. Which he then uses to buy the company.

BLOUNT: As you know, Everson Pharmaceuticals has great cash flow.

EVERSON: You're telling me he wants to take out a loan against our own cash flow and *buy us* with it?

CIZIK: Basically.

EVERSON: That's absurd.

CIZIK: The company's stock price has left you vulnerable.

EVERSON: I've got a plan to turn things around. I'm using that cash from the pharmaceuticals to renovate the mills. Once that's done, we will be able to compete with the Chinese. Revenues will recover.

BLOUNT: Shareholders won't wait.

EVERSON: Shareholders?

BLOUNT: Yes, Mr. Everson. Shareholders.

EVERSON: Do you know them? Because I don't. I don't know the person who bought stock two days ago—or two weeks ago—or two years ago. Just because you own a piece of paper does not give you the authority to know what's best for this company. We're not just some number on the exchange that makes people happy when it ticks up, and when it doesn't, makes them fuck with our lives.

CIZIK: That's the cost of going public.

EVERSON: The only reason my father ever agreed to go public was to keep the steel mills open. Yes, he took that money. And he used it to diversify. Pharmaceuticals. Financial services. Why? Because keeping those mills open, and that town employed? That's what this company is about. Making steel. You want to be a shareholder? Get on board with that vision.

CIZIK: I advised your father for twenty years. I know what's at stake.

WOMAN'S VOICE interrupts over the intercom:

INTERCOM: Mr. Everson, the car is waiting to take you to the dock. You're going to be late for the launch.

EVERSON *(To the intercom)*: Trudy. You'll have to tell the board I can't make it.

CIZIK: The board?

EVERSON: It's just an afternoon sail on the company yacht.

BLOUNT: Mr. Everson...

EVERSON: They don't actually care if I'm there.

CIZIK: You should go sailing with the board, Tom.

EVERSON: Why?

CIZIK: They have friends on the Street. You don't want them hearing about this from someone else first.

BLOUNT: You will need them if this gets ugly.

EVERSON: Absolutely absurd. Fine. I'll go.

CIZIK: Jackie and I are going to work on setting up a meeting with Peterman's people.

EVERSON: For what?

BLOUNT: To try and resolve this without going to *war*.

—SHIFT TO:

NEW YORK. LEO TRESLER'S OFFICE.

Tresler in the middle of being interviewed by Judy Chen—a financial journalist. Chen has a notepad on which she makes notes.

TRESLER: Robert Merkin is a liar and a cheat. He raises money by selling debt against a company's assets. Then he gives that money to some two-bit nobody to front the purchase. Once they own it, that company is weighed down with debt it can't pay back. That becomes the excuse for Merkin and his cronies to go in, chop it up, sell it off. He works every side of the deal. Makes fees raising the money. Makes fees lending it. Makes money off the purchase, off the sale. They can't print the bills fast enough for this racket.

CHEN: Okay.

TRESLER: You don't agree?

CHEN: You're the businessman, Mr. Tresler, I'm more interested in what *you* think Merkin is doing than—

TRESLER: *What he's doing?* What *is* he doing? We used to be a country that paid our bills. Made things. This guy comes along and says he's *manufacturing debt*. What he's making is deals that do not need to happen. Deals that are excuses for his thievery. *(Picking up a magazine)* The bastard should be arrested. Not put on the cover of *Time* magazine.

…holding up a copy of Time. *With Merkin on the cover.*

CHEN: There are a lot of very intelligent people who don't agree with you.

TRESLER: Sheep. Being led to slaughter.

CHEN: Slaughter?

TRESLER: That's where all this debt lands us sooner or later. The poorhouse.

CHEN: But hasn't American business gotten lazy? A generation of CEOs who've inherited profitable companies, happy to live like little princes, golfing at their country clubs, sailing about on their company yachts. Aren't they pretenders, Mr. Tresler?

Beat.

TRESLER: Where are you from?

CHEN: San Francisco.

TRESLER: No, I mean, you know what I mean…

CHEN: Do I?

TRESLER: You know, your parents.

CHEN: San Francisco. Born and raised.

TRESLER: Okay. Okay.

CHEN: My great-grandparents were born in China, though.

TRESLER: Right. So what'd they do?

CHEN: My great-grandfather came over to work on the railroad, actually.

TRESLER: Hardworking people. The kind who didn't take a thing for granted. Who saw the big picture and worked toward it. Not all this fake it 'til you make it.

CHEN: Decidedly not.

TRESLER: Because if that's what you're doing, faking it 'til you make it? All you know how to do once you do make it? Is fake it.

CHEN: That's novel.

TRESLER: You can have it.

CHEN: Don't worry. If I use it, I'll quote you.

TRESLER: You don't have to. That's what I'm saying...—By the way, I wish you'd call me Leo.

CHEN: Right. *(Beat)* Aren't your criticisms of Robert Merkin a little confusing—

TRESLER: Why?

CHEN: You're a very rich man. You've made a fortune doing buyouts and takeovers yourself.

TRESLER: *Friendly* takeovers. That make sense. That make a company better.

CHEN: And you use *debt* to finance some of those deals.

TRESLER: Responsibly. Not more debt than the balance sheet can afford. I work *with* management. We take a company private. We build value. Then take it public again. Six- or seven-year horizons. Nothing like what these clowns are doing. *(Picking up the magazine, leafing)* Listen to this guy: *"Debt is an asset."* *(With disgust)* Debt is not an asset. Debt is debt. *(Beat)* You know what a bond used to be when I was growing up? A way to do good. Put away a little money and help Uncle Sam in the process. I still have two twenty-five dollar Series E bonds in a box under my bed. Never cashed them. Because some part of me always felt that Uncle Sam needed it. *(Beat)* You want to write a book?

CHEN: I am writing a book, Mr. Tresler.

TRESLER: I know—I'm just saying... The book we *need* is about selfishness. People who don't care. About the country. About rules. About anything but themselves.

CHEN: So when Robert Merkin says what he's really doing—

TRESLER: You're not listening to a thing I'm saying.

CHEN: I am. And I'm writing it all down. Leo.

TRESLER: I won't hold it against you. I'd have a tough time holding anything against you...

Beat.

CHEN: Can I ask you something? Off the record?

TRESLER: Sure.

CHEN: What'd he do to you?

TRESLER: What? Who, Merkin? Nothing. Never met the guy.

Pause.

CHEN: Okay. That's good for now. If I have follow-ups...

TRESLER: Call Ellen. She'll patch you right through. Anytime.

CHEN: Thank you for your time.

TRESLER: So listen, I...—What, uh...—what's your deal?

CHEN: My deal?

TRESLER: Single, married, what?

CHEN: I'm not sure what relevance—

TRESLER: Look, let me just ask you. Just one thing. Is that okay? Without you quoting me?

CHEN: Mm-hm...

TRESLER: The interview's over, right? So, just person to person...

CHEN: Okay.

TRESLER: You ever dated a man who flew you around in a private jet?

CHEN *(Getting up to leave)*: Thank you for your time, Mr. Tresler. I appreciate the perspective you've—

TRESLER *(Coming in)*: You should try it, Judy. You really should. I think you'd like it.

CHEN: I'll reach out if I have any follow-ups.

TRESLER: I don't give up easily.

CHEN: Have a wonderful day.

> *Chen exits.*
>
> *Pause.*
>
> *Tresler considers. Then steps over to phone his secretary.*

TRESLER: Ellen.

INTERCOM: Yes, Mr. Tresler.

TRESLER: Listen. I need you to call in an order for two dozen roses. That journalist. Judy Chen. Find out where she lives and have them delivered this afternoon...

INTERCOM: What color?

TRESLER: Red, Ellen. For God's sake!

—SHIFT TO:

A BENCH.

> *And pacing around it:*
>
> *Boris Pronsky. In a black suit. With a limp. He smokes as he mutters to himself. Rehearsing his confrontation with Merkin:*

PRONSKY: I've been with you from the beginning. But you give it to him. Peterman. A nobody. Where would you be without me, Bob? Hmm? *"Boris, I made you, I made you, Boris."* *You* made me, Bob? I made *you*—

> *…when Merkin appears. Apologetic.*
>
> *Seeing the target of his ire, Pronsky seems to lose most of his bluster.*

MERKIN: Boris. Sorry I'm late.

PRONSKY: Bob.

MERKIN: Had a holdup at the office.

PRONSKY: I've been waiting a half hour. Why do we always have to meet in a park? People staring at me like I'm a pedophile.

MERKIN: You smoking again? Your kids need you.

PRONSKY: You sound like my wife.

MERKIN: Smart lady. How is Shirin?

PRONSKY: Fine.

MERKIN: Kids? Dennis?

PRONSKY: Fine.

MERKIN: He make the football team?

PRONSKY: Bob. I can't do this chitchat…I just—I can't do it—*(Tossing, putting the cigarette out underfoot)* I need to know—How could you give Everson to Peterman? Hmm? How could you give it to that nobody?

MERKIN: Boris...

PRONSKY: No, no, no. You owe me.

MERKIN: Really? Last I checked? *You* owed *me*. Six and a half million.

PRONSKY: Jesus, Bob. It's chump change to you—

MERKIN: Chump change?

PRONSKY: Don't you make *enough*?—I mean, with everything else you—

MERKIN: Boris. *I gave you* the heads up on Alliance.

PRONSKY: Because you wanted me to pump up the price.

MERKIN: Which you did. And made thirteen million doing it. I give you information—we split the take fifty-fifty. That's our agreement.

PRONSKY: I know.

MERKIN: Which means, right now, *you* owe *me* six and a half million. We're supposed to be friends, Boris. I shouldn't have to—

PRONSKY: Exactly. Friends. That's why this Peterman thing hurts so much.

MERKIN: Don't change the subject.

PRONSKY: *You* changed the subject. Only time I get calls from you anymore? When you need me to move the market—

MERKIN: How much I make you last year? Nineteen? Or twenty?

PRONSKY: Bob—

MERKIN: I make you twenty-odd million dollars and you complain?

PRONSKY: Just tell me one thing. Just one. Why him? Why not me?

MERKIN: I need someone with real balls on this.

PRONSKY: You're saying I don't have real balls—

MERKIN: I bring you deal after deal. Every time, you kick the tires 'til your foot gets sore. Then little Boris Pronsky goes home to nurse his toes in a salt bath.

PRONSKY: You never brought me a deal like Everson.

MERKIN: Rubberized was a great deal.

PRONSKY: Rubberized didn't feel right—

MERKIN: Fielding-Foster was a great deal.

PRONSKY: Didn't feel right. The deal has to feel right, Bob.

MERKIN: When you take a risk, a *real* risk? It doesn't feel *right*. Feeling *right* is about feeling *safe*. What we're doing now? Is not safe. *(Beat)* Let me bring this one in. Then you'll have your turn. Philip Morris, American Airlines...

PRONSKY: American Airlines.

MERKIN: General Electric...

PRONSKY: GE... *(Pause)* What do you need?

MERKIN: Everson. Start accumulating positions. Nothing north of forty-one. We want to bid forty-two and a half.

PRONSKY: Usual play?

MERKIN: However you want to handle it. Not too loud.

PRONSKY: GE, Bob?

MERKIN: And that check for the six and a half, Boris.

—LIGHTS OUT ON MERKIN AND PRONSKY.

—LIGHTS UP ON:

A PAY PHONE.

Pronsky picks up and dials. We hear RINGING...

—AS LIGHTS COME UP ON:

MARK O'HARE.

At an office phone. (Phones ringing in the background.)

PRONSKY: Mark, it's Boris.

O'HARE: O Prince of Darkness.

PRONSKY: Stop calling me that.

O'HARE: Then stop dressing like an undertaker.

PRONSKY: Mark.

O'HARE: Lurch.

PRONSKY: Start showing a little respect.

O'HARE: Or?

PRONSKY: Or I hang up on you.

O'HARE: I could spend the next ten minutes playing back the cassette tape I recorded of your mother howling while I fucked her in the ass and you wouldn't hang up.

PRONSKY: Turn up the volume, Mark. Still can't hear it.

O'HARE: You're a sick fuck Boris Pronsky, you know that?

PRONSKY: I'm the sick fuck who made you, Mark.

O'HARE: All right, all right.

PRONSKY: White whale. Came up for air.

O'HARE: It's about time.

PRONSKY: ESU.

O'HARE: Everson Steel?

PRONSKY: Yep.

O'HARE: What are we doing? Driving up the price and cashing out?

PRONSKY: White whale wants to eat this ship. Eat the wood on this ship.

O'HARE: A play on the Dow Jones, huh?

PRONSKY: First of many. Next one's mine. Maybe American Airlines, maybe GE.

O'HARE: Very impressive, Lurch. Very impressive.

PRONSKY: Mark. Don't call me that. I'm warning you.

O'HARE: What's the plan?

PRONSKY: Everson's trading at thirty-seven. We move it ten percent.

O'HARE: To what—forty, forty-one?

PRONSKY: Nothing north of forty-one. We want their shareholders smelling green, not seeing it.

O'HARE: Getting 'em pregnant for the takeover. Copy that.

—LIGHTS OUT ON PRONSKY.

O'Hare hangs up.

Picks up again, dials another number.

—LIGHTS UP ELSEWHERE ON:

DEVON ATKINS.

Beside him is KEVIN WALSH—Assistant to the US Attorney. Walsh is wearing headphones and is seated before a reel-to-reel recorder.

ATKINS: Atkins.

O'HARE: Dev, It's Mark.

ATKINS: Hi, Mark.

O'HARE: Can you talk?

Atkins turns to Walsh. Nods.

O'HARE (CONT'D): Dev?

Walsh snaps on the recorder switch. The wheels spin.

ATKINS: Yeah, yeah?

O'HARE: You okay over there?

ATKINS: Yeah, yeah, just eating.

O'HARE: Right. Well, I hope it's a little seafood.

ATKINS: Oh, yeah? Moby Dick?

O'HARE: Ahab finally caught sight of her.

ATKINS: Cool, cool. What's the play?

O'HARE: Ticker, ESU.

ATKINS: ESU?

O'HARE: Everson. Steel.

ATKINS: Right. Okay. Everson. Got it.

O'HARE: Nothing north of forty-one, Dev. We're just softening up the target.

ATKINS: Nothing north of forty-one.

O'HARE: We're just getting shareholders pregnant.

ATKINS: Copy that.

—LIGHTS OUT ON O'HARE.

WALSH.

Stops the reel-to-reel.

WALSH: I told you. You need to keep him on the phone longer. Get him to open up.

ATKINS: But it's just not...

WALSH: What?

ATKINS: How it goes down. When he calls. He'll suspect something. We've gotta ease into it.

WALSH: Dev, do I have to remind you that—

ATKINS: No. No. You don't.

WALSH: You need to deliver O'Hare or you're going away.

ATKINS: We just—we just have to ease into it. That's all I'm saying.

Beat.

WALSH: Ahab, huh? As in Captain.

ATKINS: It's the code. Like I told you. Ahab sees the white whale? Means the market's gonna move.

WALSH: Right.

ATKINS: Ahab doesn't want to lose his leg? Means it's time to sell.

WALSH: Ahab's only got one leg. In the book.

ATKINS: What book?

—LIGHTS OUT ON WALSH AND ATKINS.

—LIGHTS UP ON:

MERKIN HOME.

Bedroom. Merkin and his wife, Amy. Merkin holds an infant in his arms, following along as Amy explains her way through a set of spreadsheets.

AMY: Right, but when I checked again, I noticed two line items from the pharmaceutical division last year...here—*(Off another sheet)*—and here. I put those two numbers together...

MERKIN: Right...

AMY: Four years ago, that combined number was in the same ballpark as item three—*(Back on the first sheet)*—on this sheet from the steel side, *"ancillary related to overstock"*...

MERKIN: Okay.

AMY: And that was during a year when steel did similar volume.

MERKIN: I'm not following.

AMY: On *this year's* numbers from the steel division, that line item has disappeared. It's not even being entered into the spreadsheet.

MERKIN: Right?

AMY: *And*...there are new items on the pharmaceutical side labeled *"unspecified miscellaneous."* Which, when you add up...

MERKIN: Equals the number that's being erased from the steel side.

AMY: Exactly. They're breaking up losses from the steel division...

MERKIN *(Perusing)*: Taking 1.6 billion off the P&L...

AMY: Last year alone. And burying that loss in pharmaceuticals, where growth has been great—so it can take the hit.

MERKIN: Cooking the books.

AMY: Trying to make the steel division look healthier than it is. This is an even better opportunity than I realized. There's real value here. But you *have to* get rid of steel.

The baby pushes forth the first sounds of discontent. Merkin cradles and sways, trying to calm her.

MERKIN: Boy, the irony. Everson Steel is a great company, as long as you take away the steel part.

AMY: It's the truth.

MERKIN: Fine. But how's it gonna play? I mean, it's fifteen thousand jobs they're going to say *I* killed.

AMY: Bob. It was one sentence.

MERKIN: It was *Time* magazine.

AMY: Those jobs are *dying* one way or another. It's all over the P&L.

MERKIN: When it happens, that's not how they'll write it.

AMY: This country is in denial. But it won't be for much longer. *(Off the baby's worsening colic)* I think she's hungry.

Amy takes the child. Begins to feed. The baby quiets.

AMY (CONT'D): *(As she feeds)* Survival of the fittest. Creative destruction. Some things have to die for others to be born. New life. You're creating the space for new things to come into being. These are ideas people get.

Merkin is taking in the sight of his daughter and wife.

AMY: What?

MERKIN: It's all we ever really want, isn't it? To find comfort at Mommy's breast.

AMY: If it were only that simple. *(Beat)* Oh. I left an article for you on the kitchen table—from the *Journal*. About the prison sector.

MERKIN: Prison sector?

AMY: There's a company took over all the prisons in Tennessee. Started turning a profit inside of a year. Amazing margins last quarter. You wouldn't believe it. We should get in on the financing side.

MERKIN: Prisons-for-profit?

AMY: It's what's happening. For-profit prisons, for-profit schools, hospitals. Lightning growth, Bob.

MERKIN: Maybe after this Everson thing is over. *(Beat, back to the spreadsheets)* I mean, this couldn't have come at a better time. We're meeting the CEO day after tomorrow. He doesn't play ball and we leak this...?

Beat.

AMY: Are you using Boris Pronsky on this deal?

MERKIN: Ame...

AMY: Bob, you don't need him anymore.

MERKIN: I do.

AMY: You don't.

MERKIN: The system's rigged to protect the old guard. The laws are written to protect their interests. If I play by their rules, I *can't* win. You know that. So I need Boris to park stock or move the price? If that's what it takes—

AMY: You're not the underdog anymore. You're in the spotlight. You're on the cover of *Time* magazine. People are paying attention. It's time to stop.

—LIGHTS OUT ON THE MERKINS.

—LIGHTS UP FAR DOWNSTAGE ON:

TOM EVERSON.

Joined by Cizik.

CIZIK: Peterman will probably do the talking. But don't let that fool you. Merkin is very sharp. He'll be paying close attention...—Be sure to mention your plan for the low end of the steel market.

EVERSON: Why?

CIZIK: It's the kind of thing they'll understand. Common ground.

EVERSON: I'm not looking for common ground. The company is not for sale, Max. I don't even know why we're meeting these sons of bitches—

CIZIK: Tom. Peterman filed paperwork.

EVERSON: With the SEC?

CIZIK: Yes. This morning. He's buying blocks of stock.

EVERSON: Jesus. What are we doing to stop him?

CIZIK: Jackie's working on a defense. But for now, you need to be open.

EVERSON: So fucking humiliating.

—LIGHTS UP JUST BEHIND THEM SHOW:

TABLE AT LE CIRQUE.

Peterman rises as Cizik and Everson enter the light. All shake.

CIZIK: Mr. Peterman, good to see you. We've met before.

PETERMAN: Yeah, yeah. Of course. With my father.

CIZIK: How is he?

PETERMAN: Good, good. Busting everybody's balls, like usual. But he's fine. *(To Everson)* I'm Izzy Peterman.

EVERSON: Tom Everson.

CIZIK: Thanks for making the trip out from the West Coast.

PETERMAN: Love this city. Greatest city in the world.

CIZIK: Where's Bob?

PETERMAN: Always late. Get used to it.

Just as a WAITER appears.

WAITER *(In French)*: *A boire, messieurs?*

CIZIK: *Thé glacé pour moi.*

WAITER: *Parfait. (To Everson)* Usual for you, Mr. Everson?

EVERSON: Yes, Serge. Thanks.

PETERMAN: Diet Pepsi for me.

WAITER: We only have Coca-Cola.

PETERMAN: Pepsi tastes better. You know that, right?

WAITER: I'm sorry, sir.

PETERMAN: What's Coke paying you guys to keep people from making their own choice?

WAITER: Sir, I'm not the owner—

PETERMAN *(Retreating)*: Of course not and here I am giving you a rough time.

CIZIK *(Coming in, to Peterman)*: The iced tea here is not to be missed.

PETERMAN *(To the waiter)*: Okay. Give me that.

Waiter nods, exits.

PETERMAN (CONT'D): What a table, huh?

EVERSON: The Everson table.

PETERMAN: Can see the whole room. That's Gerstner over there, isn't it? Wait, is that Lee Iacocca?

CIZIK: Yes.

PETERMAN: Lee fucking Iacocca. And you guys have the best table in the house. You must do a lot of business here.

EVERSON: I do.

PETERMAN: On the company account? *(Beat)* Just kidding, Tom. I can call you Tom, right?

Just as Merkin enters…

MERKIN: Sorry I'm late. Traffic. Max?

CIZIK: Bob. Tom Everson.

MERKIN: Good to see you. I'm Bob Merkin.

Everson nods and shakes. Merkin sits.

CIZIK: So we're very excited to hear what's on your minds, gentlemen.

PETERMAN: And we're excited to tell you. I don't know how much you've heard about me—I mean—*us* at Saratoga-McDaniels—

EVERSON: Something about bowling equipment. That right, Max?

PETERMAN: It's true. *We've* gone from drugstores in Sacramento to international holdings in bowling equipment, hi-fi stereos, mint extract—

EVERSON: Mint extract?

PETERMAN: Great business. Huge demand. Only growing.

EVERSON: Right.

PETERMAN: The companies I own all share a single trait. Value. Because that's what I understand. I look at a company the way a landscaper looks at a tree. See the branches that need pruning. Others, chopping away. *Choices* like that take *courage,* Tom. That's what I bring to the table. Choice. Courage. Reform.

EVERSON: Excuse me for…—Mr. Peterman, do you know *anything* about the steel business?

PETERMAN: I know you're getting creamed. Unions, pensions, the Chinese. I know your competitors in this country are marching into Chapter Eleven. I know your father saw all this coming—

EVERSON: My *father?*

PETERMAN: Which is why he started buying businesses that had *nothing* to do with steel—

EVERSON: My father built Everson into a company that sits on the Dow Jones. And he didn't do it making bowling balls.

PETERMAN: Everyone starts somewhere.

EVERSON: Let's you and me start with the fact that my company is not for sale.

PETERMAN *(Coming in)*: Are you worried? Is that it?

EVERSON: Why would I be worried—

PETERMAN: Because if you are, I want you to know, I'm going to give you a very generous parachute package—

EVERSON: My *parachute* package—

PETERMAN: Don't get me wrong—

EVERSON *(To Cizik)*: Max, is this guy serious—

PETERMAN: I don't want you to leave.

EVERSON: You don't want me to *leave* my own company?

PETERMAN: I want you with me, Tom. In the trenches. Shoulder to shoulder. I'm just saying, *if* you're worried…

EVERSON: Why us, Mr. Peterman? Hmm? What did we do to attract your unwelcome attention? I'm fighting a battle to keep a business alive that's been in my family and in my community for three generations. Why don't you just go somewhere else? Find some other tree you can *prune*—and *piss on* to your heart's content.

CIZIK: Tom, you don't have to—

MERKIN: No, it's okay. We understand. This is very emotional. *(Turning to Peterman)* Izzy, do you mind…? *(Beat)* Mr. Everson. With due respect, we all live in the market. Respond to the market. Grow with the market. The market is the rule of our being. Those who don't obey, well, they begin to lag. And when they lag, they draw notice. Because they're weak. And the weak are, eventually, consumed. *(Beat)* Sometimes a company can *hide* that weakness—with accounting tricks. Declaring losses, say, from one division against profits in another. And it can buy time. But eventually the truth comes out.

EVERSON: Are you threatening me?

MERKIN: On the contrary. I'm saying Everson Steel has a great future. But that future is not *in* steel. And you seem to be the only one who doesn't get that.

EVERSON: Thank you for the lesson. I've heard a great deal about you. None of it positive.

CIZIK: He doesn't really mean that—

EVERSON: Oh, I do. *(Getting up)* Sorry to disappoint you both, concerned as you seem to be for my company. Which, as I said earlier, is not for sale.

PETERMAN: At close of market today, I will be a seven percent shareholder.

EVERSON: Which leaves you a lot of ground to make up before you get anywhere near fifty-one percent. *(To Cizik)* Let's go, Max.

PETERMAN: I'll bid in the low-forties. And I will go up from there.

EVERSON: Have at it.

PETERMAN: When shareholders see that price rising—

EVERSON: Shareholders?

PETERMAN: They will side with me.

EVERSON: Fuck the shareholder.

PETERMAN: Pretty much sums *you* up, doesn't it?

EVERSON: And fuck you.

Everson walks out.

Leaving Cizik behind. Who gets up. Just as the waiter enters with the drinks.

CIZIK: Uh, thank you, gentlemen, for a—

MERKIN: It's okay, Max. Nobody took it personally.

CIZIK: Well, I think he may have. *(Placing his napkin on the table)* I wish you both a good day.

Cizik exits.

—SHIFT TO:

THE US ATTORNEY'S OFFICE.

Giuseppe Addesso, the US Attorney for the Southern District of New York. With Kevin Walsh—whom we've thus far seen in a scene with Atkins.

WALSH: You know how long this kind of thing can take. Took you three years before you even got to Luchese's capo.

ADDESSO: That was worth it.

WALSH: Papers loved it—

ADDESSO: A service to the community.

WALSH: And the papers loved you. US Attorney, Italian-American, going after Italian-American organized crime.

ADDESSO: First and foremost a service to the community.

WALSH: So is this.

ADDESSO: I'm not sure I see that. I'm not sure anybody does.

WALSH: These are not victimless crimes, Joe. The victim here is the system. And that's gonna have—

ADDESSO: Kevin. Seven months you've been working on this. All you've got are small fry. You're not keeping this alive with speeches anymore.

WALSH: I'm onto something. Finally.

ADDESSO: This kid, Atkins? It's not enough.

WALSH: I just got up on him and he's already got me onto another target. O'Hare. Mark O'Hare.

ADDESSO: Never heard of him.

WALSH: O'Hare does big volume. A lot of short selling.

ADDESSO: *Short selling?*

WALSH: How you make money when prices fall.

ADDESSO: Nobody understands this shit. Nobody cares about it.

WALSH: You mean the papers don't care about it.

ADDESSO: You're right. They don't. And maybe they're right not to.

Pause.

WALSH: These guys have a code. Losing legs, eating ships. Someone they're calling the white whale is at the top. O'Hare is connected to a guy they're calling Ahab. Ahab knows the white whale.

ADDESSO: Ahab—as in Captain?

WALSH: That's what I'm saying. There's a big fish here. There has to be. Let me stay up on this.

ADDESSO: Warrant gives you another thirty days. But I can't afford another thirty—

WALSH: Joe. I need more time.

ADDESSO: What is this about for you? What do you get from this?

WALSH: Can't I just want to do my job? You really don't understand that?

ADDESSO: Two weeks. That's what you've got. Then I'm pulling the plug.

—SHIFT TO:

EVERSON HEADQUARTERS.

Everson, Cizik, and Blount—who is handing out papers.
Everson takes one. Agitated.

EVERSON: Eleven percent? Peterman's at *eleven* percent?

CIZIK: As of this morning.

EVERSON: How?

CIZIK: He's buying shares in the open market. We can't stop him from doing that.

BLOUNT: Yet. We can't stop him *yet*. *(Indicating the paper)* But this will.

EVERSON: What is it?

BLOUNT: A poison pill. A defensive tactic that allows management to—

EVERSON: I know what a poison pill is.

BLOUNT: I didn't mean to—

EVERSON: How old are you again?

BLOUNT: I'm not sure what that has to—

CIZIK *(Coming in)*: She's twenty-eight.

EVERSON: Right.

BLOUNT: Is there a problem?

EVERSON: No. I just...A little experience in this matter, Max— might make me feel...I don't know—

CIZIK: Jackie's the best we've got. Top of her class, Harvard Law.

BLOUNT: Harvard College. Harvard Business. Harvard Law.

CIZIK: She's been with us three years. She understands this terrain better than anyone at Lausanne & Company.

EVERSON: Wonder Woman. Got it.

BLOUNT: We structure the pill as follows: If anyone succeeds in acquiring more than twenty percent of Everson Steel—

CIZIK: Meaning Peterman.

BLOUNT: Right, but we can't say that.

EVERSON: Okay.

BLOUNT: If anyone gets to twenty percent, all *current* shareholders automatically swap their shares—

EVERSON: Swap?

BLOUNT: For fifty-seven dollars.

EVERSON: With what?

BLOUNT: Debt. We were thinking one-year bonds.

EVERSON: Paid by who?

BLOUNT: Well, the company, sir.

EVERSON: Me.

CIZIK: We're not expecting it to get that far.

BLOUNT: Because with the pill in place, should Peterman *get* to twenty percent, the stock price would jump from forty dollars—where it is this morning—to *fifty-seven*. A forty percent price hike. That's the poison.

CIZIK: He bites that pill, he goes "boom."

Beat.

EVERSON: You're saying that if he acquires twenty percent, the price jumps to fifty-seven...

BLOUNT: Exactly.

EVERSON: But only because *we're* agreeing to buy everybody's shares at that price?

BLOUNT: Yes.

EVERSON: So then don't *we* go "boom"?

BLOUNT: That's not the point.

EVERSON: Oh, right. Sorry to have missed that.

BLOUNT: The pill's a deterrent.

CIZIK: Peterman will litigate. The real point here is to buy time.

EVERSON: Time for what?

BLOUNT: To craft a counteroffer to shareholders.

EVERSON: Fucking shareholders.

BLOUNT: Whether you like it or not, the company's in play. Somebody will buy it. That buyer might as well be you.

EVERSON: I already own it!

CIZIK: Not for much longer. Not if you don't do something.

EVERSON: Buying back shares at fifty-seven is untenable—

BLOUNT: That's not—

EVERSON *(Over)*: We can't afford it at *forty!* We couldn't afford it at thirty-five!

BLOUNT: We can do a lot with debt these days. Selling junk in Everson Steel would allow you—

EVERSON: Debt like that will kill this company! Every cent we make'll be siphoned off to pay down debt. We need that money to renovate the mills. We can't do this.

CIZIK: Then we need to find someone with the muscle to do it *without* junk.

—LIGHTS SHIFT TO SHOW ONLY:

BLOUNT.

On a phone.

—AND LIGHTS UP ELSEWHERE ON:

RIVERA.

On a phone as well. Making notes.

BLOUNT: We're going to stop the deal with a poison pill.

RIVERA: Not bad. How's it structured?

BLOUNT: Fifty-seven dollars a share once Peterman gets to twenty percent.

RIVERA: Cash?

BLOUNT: Debt.

RIVERA: Oh. We win that.

BLOUNT: You'll have to litigate. The pill buys us time.

RIVERA: For what?

BLOUNT: To court a white-knight buyer.

RIVERA: Yeah, right.

BLOUNT: Max wants to go to Tresler.

RIVERA: Leo Tresler? That fucking windbag?

BLOUNT: Very *rich* fucking windbag. He's a good businessman, Raúl.

RIVERA: At these price levels? Whoever buys it has to come to Bob for the money. He's the only guy can raise this kind of dough.

BLOUNT: Everson is not coming to you. First City would *kill* to do a deal like this. We're talking fifty, seventy million dollars in fees...

RIVERA: We made this game, Jackie. I know what the fees are.

BLOUNT: You're doing so well, Raúl, why don't you pick up a tab every now and then?

RIVERA: Whatever.

BLOUNT: Just because you guys started this game, doesn't mean you own it. Everybody wants in now.

RIVERA: So why are you talking to me about this deal? I mean you're not *supposed* to be talking to me. If it's not about trying to get a deal done with us.

BLOUNT: That *is* what it's about.

RIVERA: Because if you're getting cold feet about being my little mole…

BLOUNT: I need to learn how to do these deals, Raúl. Max doesn't have a clue. I need the front-row seat. *(Off a sudden thought)* Oh, by the way, we're going to sue you guys for records. Looking for disclosure violations.

RIVERA: Mmm-hmm.

BLOUNT: Which means subpoenas are coming.

RIVERA: Well, we don't have a thing.

BLOUNT: Of course not.

RIVERA: But thanks. Gotta go.

—LIGHTS UP ON:

MERKIN AT HIS DESK.

Rivera walks in.

RIVERA: Just got off the phone with my mole at Everson.

MERKIN: And?

RIVERA: Poison pill.

MERKIN: Predictable.

RIVERA: *And* they're going to an outside buyer.

MERKIN: Who?

RIVERA: Leo Tresler.

MERKIN: Not worried.

RIVERA: *And* they're going to sue us for records.

This gets Merkin's attention.

MERKIN: For what?

RIVERA: To look for disclosure violations.

MERKIN: That's not good.

RIVERA: We just get rid of the evidence before they subpoena.

MERKIN: Okay, great.

RIVERA: It's just...

MERKIN: What?

RIVERA: I'm your lawyer, Bob. You don't want your lawyer to have blood on his hands.

MERKIN: Raúl, I pay you not to tell me things like this.

RIVERA: I get that—but—

MERKIN: Okay. Fine. Get Charlene to do it.

Pause. Rivera nods.

—LIGHTS UP SOMEWHERE FAR UPSTAGE ON:

DOCUMENT SHREDDER.

As lights animate the area, Merkin's assistant, CHAR-LENE, turns on the shredder.

Rivera steps in, begins to "explain"—which we don't hear—as Charlene now shreds documents.

The shredding continues as we...

—RETURN TO:

MERKIN'S OFFICE.

Peterman has now joined, with the newspaper. Pacing as he reads and talks. Merkin continuing to do math on a pad.

PETERMAN: You see Levine? In the *Wall Street Journal*? Talking about us?

MERKIN: No, what?

PETERMAN: Front page. Quote — "One hopes the American public will understand these brash, young Jewish financiers do not represent all Jews in America. Their greed is their own." — End quote.

MERKIN: Levine's a stooge for those blue bloods. He's playing right into what they want to hear. Because when those white-shoe guys go out there and win? When *they* take the spoils? Then it's life, liberty, and the pursuit of happiness. When *we* do it? Suddenly it's *greed*. Or when guys like Raúl do it? It's foreigners buying up our country.

PETERMAN: Yeah, but this is Levine, Bob. He's one of us.

MERKIN: He's not one of us. He's a dinosaur.

PETERMAN: Still. I mean...

MERKIN: Didn't his parents die in Auschwitz or something?

PETERMAN: Not just his parents. I think it was like everyone on both sides.

MERKIN: Guys like that are always listening for the ovens to be lit up again. They're living in fear, Iz.

Just as Rivera returns.

RIVERA: Done, Bob.

MERKIN: Raúl. What'd your mole say was the price on the poison pill?

RIVERA: Fifty-seven.

MERKIN *(Noting, calculating)*: Fifty-seven means...

PETERMAN *(Worried, over)*: That's more than a third higher.

MERKIN *(Finishing the math)*: Two point two billion...

PETERMAN: Jesus.

MERKIN: We're closing in on two billion as it is. We'll hit the phones. Sell more bonds.

RIVERA: Some poison pill *that* is.

MERKIN: More like a chewable vitamin.

RIVERA: Gummy bear.

PETERMAN: Bob.

MERKIN: What?

PETERMAN: That's a lot of debt.

MERKIN: What do you care?

Rivera continues:

RIVERA: By the way...

PETERMAN: What?

RIVERA: Get your people to erase all trace of Veronica pre-August.

PETERMAN: Why?

RIVERA: My mole says they're preparing to sue.

PETERMAN: For what?

RIVERA: Disclosure violations.

PETERMAN: I fucking told you.

RIVERA: It'll be fine.

PETERMAN: Fine? It's *my* ass'll be hung out to dry—

RIVERA: Nobody's ass is getting hung out—

PETERMAN: You fucking people.

RIVERA: Just make the calls.

MERKIN: Take care of it.

—LIGHTS OUT.

—A LIGHT SHOWS:

MERKIN.

On a phone.

—AND A LIGHT OPPOSITE SHOWS:

PRONSKY.

Picking up.

PRONSKY: Pronsky.

MERKIN: Boris, it's Bob. We've got a problem.

PRONSKY: What'd I do now?

MERKIN: No. Everson Steel. Management's having trouble seeing reason. They're going to fight us.

PRONSKY: Okay...

MERKIN: I think it's time they felt a little of the Pronsky pain.

PRONSKY: How much?

MERKIN: A pipe. Across the knees.

PRONSKY: You want me to unload the positions?

MERKIN: Every share. I want to see that stock price nose-dive. Hard.

PRONSKY: Done.

—LIGHTS OUT ON MERKIN.

PRONSKY.

Hangs up. Then dials.

—LIGHTS UP ON:

O'HARE.

PRONSKY: Mark.

O'HARE: Lurch.

PRONSKY: Jesus, Mark.

O'HARE: All right, all right.

PRONSKY: I've got news. From the white whale.

O'HARE: Thar she blows.

PRONSKY: Everson Steel.

O'HARE: Tell me something I don't know. I'm sitting on a percent and a quarter of this fucker.

PRONSKY: Well you better start selling.

O'HARE: Why?

PRONSKY: Just do it.

O'HARE: Whoa, whoa, whoa. I'm not your lapdog, Boris.

PRONSKY: I'm doing you a favor.

O'HARE: Tell me what's going on?

PRONSKY: What's going on is you locking in your profits or losing them.

O'HARE: What'd the white whale say? Is Everson happening or not?

PRONSKY: Sell, Mark.

Beat.

O'HARE: I see.

PRONSKY: What do you see?

O'HARE: I see you taking Moby's dick like the prison bitch that you are.

PRONSKY: Mark. Sell.

O'HARE: Fuck you, Boris.

PRONSKY: Or don't. I don't give a shit.

Pronsky hangs up.

—LIGHTS OUT ON PRONSKY.

O'HARE.

Dials another number.

—LIGHTS UP ON:

ATKINS.

And Walsh, beside him—in headphones, with the reel-to-reel recorder.

ATKINS: Atkins.

O'HARE: Dev, Dev, Dev.

ATKINS: Hey, Mark.

Atkins nods at Walsh. Walsh snaps on the recorder. The wheels turn.

O'HARE: News from Ahab.

ATKINS: What is it?

O'HARE: In a fucking lather over Everson Steel.

ATKINS: Okay.

O'HARE: Worried about losing that leg.

ATKINS: Start selling?

O'HARE: Lickety-split.

ATKINS: So the takeover's off?

O'HARE: That's the word.

ATKINS: Are we dumping it?

O'HARE: Every share.

ATKINS: Dumping Everson. Got it.

Walsh shoots Atkins a look. Prodding, annoyed.

ATKINS (CONT'D): Mark, Mark. Before you go...

O'HARE: What is it?

ATKINS: Um...—who's Ahab?

O'HARE: 'Scuse me?

ATKINS: I don't know. I was just hearing some things. I don't know...You know...About CEOs and stuff.

O'HARE: CEOs?

ATKINS: It was this article. About how some of them try to get rich off information, and—

O'HARE: Dev.

ATKINS: You know, so it just got me wondering about Ahab, that maybe he was someone like that—

O'HARE: Dev.

ATKINS: What?

O'HARE: Shut up. *(Off Atkins's silence)* Am I making you money or not?

ATKINS: No, you are. Mark. Definitely.

O'HARE: So stop with the fucking questions, and just get on with it. Liquidate. Everson.

ATKINS: Roger that.

—SHIFT TO:

EVERSON.

—WITH:

CIZIK.

EVERSON: Good God, Max. What is going on? The stock price is down twelve percent in two hours. Board members are calling me in a panic.

CIZIK: Traders on the Street are spreading rumors the deal is dead.

EVERSON: What *deal?*

CIZIK: Tom. Get your head out of the sand. Ignoring this is not going to make it go away.

EVERSON: What are you doing to stop it?

CIZIK: Jackie is still working on the poison pill. I'm meeting with Tresler in an hour. We're making progress. He's interested.

EVERSON: Fucking nightmare in real time.

—LIGHTS SHIFT TO:

TRESLER'S OFFICE.

Tresler with Cizik.

TRESLER: Down twelve percent.

CIZIK: Last I checked.

TRESLER: Which puts pressure on Tom to agree to a takeover just to get the stock price moving back up.

CIZIK: Basically.

TRESLER: Merkin's putting the screws to you. You won't play ball? This is what it feels like when you don't do what he wants. When are people going to wake up to this guy?

CIZIK: He makes the market, Leo—

TRESLER: He doesn't *make* the market. He IS the market. Bob Merkin is the bond market, and if somebody doesn't do something, he'll become the equities market, and before we know it, he'll own the goddamn country. Don't get me started—

CIZIK: Okay—

TRESLER: Before Merkin? You think anybody even knew what that shit was? It was exactly what they call it. Junk. Nobody had it, nobody wanted it. Then along comes this shyster.

CIZIK: Leo—

TRESLER: Making crummy loans to worthless companies like *Saratoga-McDaniels* so he can sell his crazy paper.

CIZIK: I thought you didn't want—

TRESLER: This guy, Peterman? *Israel* Peterman? I mean who is this guy? Bowling balls? And they're going to raise him two billion dollars to keep this leechfest going? Merkin is changing the climate. Mark my words, Max: Unchecked, that Shylock will destroy this country.

CIZIK: That's enough.

TRESLER: What?

CIZIK: With me? It's fine—

TRESLER: What's fine?

CIZIK: Say what you want. But out there?

TRESLER: What the hell are you talking about?

CIZIK: Shylock? Shyster?

TRESLER: That's what he is.

CIZIK: Find a different name for it—

TRESLER: Max. The guy gives good Jews like you a bad name.

CIZIK: Good Jews?

TRESLER: Yeah.

CIZIK: Just stop.

TRESLER: Don't get all uptight with me.

CIZIK: Leo.

TRESLER: Don't be one of these *overly sensitive*—

CIZIK: You're a good businessman. Let's keep it to business. Everson Steel wants you. Tom has a vision for the company. He can turn it around. He just needs time. You getting involved gives him that.

Tresler's desk intercom interrupts.

INTERCOM: Sir...

TRESLER: Sorry. Hold on. *(Into the intercom)* Yeah...

INTERCOM: Judy Chen for you?

TRESLER: Put her through. *(Picking up the phone)* Judy, hi...

—LIGHTS UP ON CHEN.

On the phone.

CHEN: Mr. Tresler. I got your message. I'd love to join you.

TRESLER: Great, great.

CHEN: Business? Cocktail? Formal?

TRESLER: Formal. I'll have a car waiting outside your place at six
thirty.

CHEN: See you then.

TRESLER: Looking forward to it.

—LIGHTS OUT ON CHEN.

BACK TO TRESLER AND CIZIK.

TRESLER (CONT'D): *(Turning to Cizik)* What really worries me,
Max—even good banks like Lausanne & Company, even
you will be tempted. There's too much money to be made
for you to stay on the sidelines much longer.

CIZIK: It's not going to happen. It's not. Trust me.

Beat.

TRESLER: I'm open to doing a deal. But no junk. I am not financing a deal with junk.

—LIGHTS SHIFT AS CIZIK EXITS.

TRESLER ALONE.

Thinking.
He walks behind his desk and presses the intercom.

TRESLER: Ellen.

ELLEN: Yes, Mr. Tresler?

TRESLER: Call the US Attorney's office. Get me some time with
Joe. Drinks, lunch, whatever works for him.

—TRANSITION TO:

JUDY CHEN.

Addressing the audience.

CHEN: Access. I wanted access. *(Beat)* Tresler took me to the Metropolitan Club that night, where the Walter Wristons and Brooke Astors were rubbing shoulders and trading blandishments with then little-known nebbishes like Alan Greenspan. But I was surprised to find painters and poets— even playwrights— "working" the room. The age of speaking truth to power seemed to be coming to an end. But the book I wanted to write was taking shape inside me, and in it, I would torpedo every piety of this new faux-religion of finance. *(Beat)* On the way out that night I passed the great Joan Didion. She was arguing with a broad dour bald man. The name Robert Merkin was going back and forth between them. He thought Merkin a visionary, paving the way to a new Jerusalem. Didion laughed so hard she spit out her drink. Merkin was the name on everyone's lips. I'd been trying for months to get an interview. I lingered in the foyer until Didion was done, and then I approached the dour man myself. I asked if he knew Merkin personally. He did. Merkin's junk had financed his latest skyscraper—a much-reviled new eyesore on Third Avenue. I begged for an introduction. He took my card. The next day, Merkin's office called. Access, indeed...

—SHE WALKS INTO:

CHEN/MERKIN INTERVIEW.

MERKIN: Take the Latino-American community. A more driven, intelligent, enterprising people you will not find. They make America stronger, better. But then you see the awful statistics. Latino-owned businesses receiving almost no corporate seed money, no financing. Why do you think that is?

CHEN: You're suggesting ethnic prejudice in corporate America?

MERKIN: No less than anywhere else in our society. And I'm also saying, that the only real way to neutralize prejudice of that sort? Wealth. Because wealth is the great equalizer in American life.

Chen notes. Then shifts.

CHEN: You have called debt an asset.

MERKIN: I have.

CHEN: To a lot of people, that idea of debt having value is confusing.

MERKIN: What is debt, but the promise to pay? From that promise, everything else flows. Debt is the nothing that gives birth to everything.

CHEN: That's very abstract.

MERKIN: Is it? What's money? Debt on a piece of paper. That's all a dollar bill is. The US government's promise on paper to honor the face value of this debt.

CHEN: Right.

MERKIN: And how does the US government honor that debt?

CHEN: Are you asking me?

MERKIN: I am.

CHEN: It sells Treasury Bonds.

MERKIN: It sells debt to honor debt. Uncle Sam sells bonds to create money. That's what we're doing. Selling bonds to create value.

CHEN: You're comparing yourself with the US government, Mr. Merkin.

MERKIN: Actually, I'm saying *we're* doing a better job than the US government.

—LIGHTS SHIFT/CROSS TO:

A BAR.

Tresler and Addesso sitting side by side. In suits. With midday martinis before them.

TRESLER: Don't kid yourself. D'Amaso's gonna pick his own successor.

ADDESSO: He's freezing me out.

TRESLER: Because you're a threat. But he's got the Republican machine on his side. You want it? You'll end up having to take on the party.

ADDESSO: I know.

TRESLER: With the track record you're building? Don't endanger it. You're a winner. Don't give them a loss to hang around your neck.

ADDESSO: What my wife keeps telling me.

TRESLER: Fuck the Senate. Fuck the Senate when there's the mayor's race. From US Attorney for the Southern District to Gracie Mansion.

ADDESSO: It does sound nice.

TRESLER: It's a no-brainer. I have a lot of friends in this town, Joe. I could raise money for that with my hands tied behind my back.

ADDESSO: Behind your back?

TRESLER: With my hands tied.

—CROSS/BACK TO:

INTERVIEW.

MERKIN: Because debt is power.

CHEN: How so?

MERKIN: Debt forces discipline. Clear decision making. Think about it from your own life. That monthly payment on the car, the house. You pay those bills before everything else, right?

CHEN: I do.

MERKIN: You budget around that number. You make adjustments to your lifestyle around that number. It's the same with a company's debt load. It cuts through delusion. It clarifies. Cleanses the balance sheet of everything unnecessary.

CHEN: Then why do you think there's such resistance?

MERKIN: From the day we're born, what do we hear? Saving is good. Borrowing is bad. Don't get into debt. But it's all backwards, isn't it?

CHEN: In what way?

MERKIN: Debt signifies new beginnings. You borrow money to do something, build something, start anew. What if we stopped being so ashamed of it? The wealth we would generate? Good God. We would create a new America.

—CROSS/BACK TO:

BAR.

ADDESSO: All right, all right. I get it.

TRESLER: Get what?

ADDESSO: You want something. What is it?

TRESLER: Joe. I'm a supporter.

ADDESSO: I know you are. And I know you want something. Cough it up. If I can help, Leo, you know I will...

Pause.

TRESLER: Didn't you tell me that you guys were working on some Wall Street things?

ADDESSO: Cases?

TRESLER: Yeah. You come up with anything?

ADDESSO: I can't discuss that with you Leo, c'mon.

TRESLER: But I can discuss it with you. Right?

—CROSS/BACK TO:

INTERVIEW.

CHEN: But what happens when this debt you're creating starts defaulting?

MERKIN: We've been doing it fifteen years. Hasn't happened yet.

CHEN: But it could.

MERKIN: It's a risk worth taking. We can't live our lives in fear, Ms. Chen. I watched my father do that his whole life. And I saw his passion dry up. I saw him shrivel away.

CHEN: Your father was an accountant.

MERKIN: Yes, he was. He taught me a lot. Except about risk. And I get it. He had it hard. But hardship can't be an excuse to let people stop you.

CHEN: Stop you from what?

MERKIN: From becoming whoever it is you want to be.

—CROSS/BACK TO:

BAR.

TRESLER: People don't like him, Joe. They want to see him stopped.

ADDESSO: Leo. Buyouts are legal, junk or no junk. I don't know what you want me to tell you.

TRESLER: The deals this guy's doing are different.

ADDESSO: How?

TRESLER: They're big. Too big. His latest scheme? He's trying to take over Everson Steel. If he gets it, that's ten, fifteen thousand jobs gone, right there. And there's no telling where it stops. Because once he's on the Dow, he'll be a stone's throw to Boeing, Alcoa, Westinghouse. American manufacturing.

ADDESSO: Everson Steel?

TRESLER: The Dow Jones. Joe, it's David against Goliath. The only way David wins? Breaking the rules.

—CROSS/BACK TO:

INTERVIEW.

CHEN: Your critics believe you bend the rules. That you'll do anything to get a deal done.

MERKIN: I think that's true.

CHEN: Do you break the law?

MERKIN: Excuse me?

CHEN: Do you break the law to get deals done?

MERKIN: Absolutely not.

CHEN: Do you use proxies in the marketplace to force the conditions for a takeover?

MERKIN: No.

CHEN: So the rumors of you leaking information to manipulate stock price—

MERKIN: Patently false.

—CROSS/BACK TO:

BAR.

ADDESSO: Leaking information?

TRESLER: And trading on that information.

ADDESSO: Insider trading...

TRESLER: Run amok, Joe. Run amok. They're no better than racketeers.

ADDESSO: Racketeers.

TRESLER: That's how a guy like this is vulnerable.

ADDESSO: Everson Steel?

TRESLER: Ticker symbol, ESU.

ADDESSO: What'd this Merkin guy do to you, Leo?

TRESLER: To me? Look at what he's doing to the country.

ADDESSO: Sounds like he did something to you.

TRESLER: ESU, Joe. Everson Steel.

ADDESSO: I heard you.

TRESLER: Last I heard, you were the US Attorney for the Southern District. Just trying to help you do your job.

—CROSS/BACK TO:

INTERVIEW.

CHEN: Do you have secret ownership stakes in the companies you finance?

MERKIN: No.

CHEN: Is it true you made eight hundred million dollars before taxes last year?

MERKIN: Can we go off the record?

CHEN: Sure.

MERKIN: I don't like the direction of your questions. Or your tone.

CHEN: Are we back on the record? *(Beat)* No one in American history has ever made that much money in a single year— other than Al Capone. Any comment?

MERKIN: We're done here. My assistant will show you out.

Merkin exits.

—LIGHTS SHIFT TO SHOW:

EVERSON.

On the floor of the steel mill in Allegheny, Pennsylvania. A union rep in a hard hat stands before Everson...

UNION REP: Okay, simmer down out there. I want you all to show a little quiet and a little respect here. Been a lot of rumors going around, so Mr. Everson's decided to speak to some of what's going on. *(Suddenly)* Jessie, if you don't stop yapping over there... Okay. Tom?

EVERSON: Thank you, Alex. Good to be with you folks. Look, I know we've had our problems over the years. You've had problems with my father, with his father, with me. We've been on opposite sides of a lot of things. They used to say there was a picture of my dad in the locker room folks used to stick their gum on, and they probably did worse than that. I know you're hearing rumors. And I know you're worried. About your jobs. About the mills. I'd understand if you felt helpless. *(Beat)* I remember the first time my dad brought me to this mill. I was seven. Standing on the bridge there, just as they were starting to pour the molten iron into the furnace. I had the goggles on, hard hat, the works. I remember seeing those huge metal arms moving around like something out of science fiction. The molten iron spilling into the cradle, the rim crowned with sparks. Liquid lightning, my dad used to call it. He turned to me, and he said: Son, one day, all this? It'll be your job to take care of it. *(Beat)* You're family to us. You're family to me. You always have been. For all our differences, different sides of the fence, and all that, we've always been united on two things. Jobs and steel.

WORKER: That why you keep cutting our wages? Because we're like family to you?

UNION REP: Sean. A little respect.

EVERSON: These are troubled times. I won't lie to you. But my dad always used to say where there's a problem, there's a solution. We are going to solve this. I promise you, each and every one of you: I'm going to keep these doors open and keep you all pouring liquid lightning for as long as I'm on this planet. And hopefully a lot longer than that.

—SHIFT TO:

MERKIN AND HIS WIFE.

At home. The television's on. He's worked up.

MERKIN: Then she compared me to Al Capone.

AMY: How?

MERKIN: Saying that that's the only person who'd made more money in a single year in American history.

AMY: She knew how much we made?

MERKIN: She thought she did. She wasn't even close. *(Beat)* This is why I don't want to talk to the press. Mindless. Repeating the same puritanical crap. Rich is bad—we're obsessed with it, we can't get enough of it—but it's bad. Poor is good—we don't want to have a damn thing to do with it, God forbid we end up poor—but it's good. Brain dead.

AMY: Comparing you to Capone is ridiculous.

MERKIN: Ridiculous or not, she puts it in print? Then it's out there.

AMY: For people to chuckle at.

MERKIN: She went after me about the equity warrants. She asked if we had ownership in the takeover targets.

AMY: We do.

MERKIN: I told her we didn't.

AMY: Why?

MERKIN: There's no way for her to prove it. She can't know what's in our private accounts.

AMY: You're financing the companies. You have the right to equity. J.P. Morgan did the same thing.

MERKIN: And he kept it quiet, too.

AMY: There's nothing illegal. You don't need to lie about it —

MERKIN *(Coming in)*: People will think I'm trying to buy every-thing. That I'm trying to buy the country. They'll think —

AMY: You're creating all this wealth. For everyone. For the coun-try. You're entitled to your part.

MERKIN: You don't think it makes me look greedy?

Beat.

AMY: You need to be stronger.

MERKIN: What is that supposed to mean?

AMY: You know what you're up against. Better than anyone. They don't want you to win. But you will. Because you are stronger.

MERKIN: I'm not feeling stronger right now.

AMY: Fine.

MERKIN: Fine, what?

AMY: Fine. You want me to leave you alone so you can sulk, I will. You want me to tell you it's all going to end well? I will. You want me to hold your head while you cry into my lap, I'll do that, too. But whatever I do? When I'm done doing it, nothing changes. You will still need to be stronger.

Pause.

MERKIN: I know.

AMY: What you're feeling is not their mindlessness. It's their envy. And you know what? There's nothing wrong with it. They're looking at you and seeing what they want. It's nor-mal. It's American.

—INTERCUT:

ADDESSO AND WALSH.

On phones.

WALSH: Walsh.

ADDESSO: Kevin. That kid you've got on the wire?

WALSH: Atkins.

ADDESSO: Right, Atkins—

WALSH: I'm making headway, Joe. I'm hoping to have—

ADDESSO: On the calls you're monitoring, you ever hear anything about Everson?

WALSH: Everson Steel? Sure.

ADDESSO: What?

WALSH: They've been yapping about it for weeks. They were buying it. Then they dumped it. Now they're buying it again.

ADDESSO: They're buying it again?

WALSH: As of a few days ago.

ADDESSO: Same ring?

WALSH: And the information's coming from the guy they're calling Ahab.

ADDESSO: Ahab.

WALSH: As in Captain. *Moby Dick?* That's where Ahab comes from. Remember, I was saying, they have a code—

ADDESSO: I've read *Moby Dick,* Kevin.

WALSH: I just thought—

ADDESSO: For God's sake.

WALSH: Sorry.

ADDESSO: Who's the guy Atkins is talking to?

WALSH: A guy named O'Hare. Mark O'Hare.

ADDESSO *(Beat)*: You have enough to bring him in?

WALSH: For a case? I don't know.

ADDESSO: Enough to scare him into talking?

WALSH: I think so.

ADDESSO: Okay. Let's start pulling on this Everson thread. Let's see what comes undone.

—RESUME:

MERKIN HOME.

Their phone rings. Twice. Then Amy's voice:

AMY/ANSWERING MACHINE: Hi. We're not home. Leave a message at the beep.

We hear Pronsky:

PRONSKY: Bob. I don't know where you are. I've been trying to reach out. I'm in LA. I'm at the Bel-Air. Call me.

Then a dial tone. Then silence.

AMY: Second time he's called. What's going on?

MERKIN: That's just Boris.

AMY: What's he calling about?

MERKIN: No idea.

Again, the phone rings.
Another ring.

AMY/ANSWERING MACHINE: Hi. We're not home. Leave a message at the beep.

PRONSKY: Bob. They fucked up my reservation. I'm gonna change hotels. Call me at the Peninsula. Call me.

Merkin doesn't get up to get the phone. They kiss.

AMY: You doing business with him?

MERKIN: Ame...

AMY: What is it with you and this guy Bob? Can you just not control yourself? I mean, what is it?

MERKIN: Amy. He's just calling. I have no idea what he wants.

AMY: You're not doing business with him?

MERKIN: I'm not doing business with Boris. I promise.

—SHIFT TO:

A BENCH.

Twilight.

In the fading day, Boris Pronsky paces just as he did earlier in the act. Smoking.

Merkin appears in the wings. Silent. He approaches Pronsky. Something dark about his advance. Almost as if moving toward an assignation.

Pronsky pulls something from his coat. A check. Hands it to Merkin, who takes it.

MERKIN: Six and a half.

PRONSKY: Told you I was good for it.

MERKIN: Don't call the house anymore. I told you before.

PRONSKY: I couldn't reach you at the office.

MERKIN: Don't. Call. The house.

PRONSKY: Fine.

MERKIN: This Everson thing is about to get ugly.

PRONSKY: It's already been messy.

MERKIN: It's going to get worse. What are you up?

PRONSKY: Up?

MERKIN: On your Everson trades so far? Two, two and a half?

PRONSKY: You keeping track?

MERKIN: Half what you make trading on information is mine—

PRONSKY: I just gave you a check for—

MERKIN: For the *last* deal. That was for *that* deal. I'm talking about *this* deal.

PRONSKY: Fine.

MERKIN: Fine?

PRONSKY: No, I mean…Of course. I'm good for it. You know that.

MERKIN: Do I?

PRONSKY: I owe you everything, Bob. You know that.

MERKIN: Then say it.

PRONSKY: You made me.

MERKIN: Again.

PRONSKY: You made me, Bob. You make us all.

Merkin stares at him for a silent beat.

MERKIN: American Airlines.

PRONSKY: That the next one?

MERKIN: American Express.

PRONSKY: Jesus.

MERKIN: Goodyear. Kodak. Ford.

PRONSKY: Ford? Fuck.

MERKIN: Chevron…

PRONSKY: Exxon?

MERKIN: Texaco.

PRONSKY: What about GM, Bob?

MERKIN: GM, GE…

PRONSKY: Good God.

MERKIN: Merck, McDonald's, Minnesota Mining.

PRONSKY: So, like, the whole Dow?

MERKIN: The whole Dow.

PRONSKY: God. Oh, God.

MERKIN: We're going to take it all.

END OF ACT ONE.

Act Two

A VOICE:

MAN (VOICEOVER): Welcome to the keynote session of this year's Private Investor Conference. Our speaker truly needs no introduction. He's the reason we're here. He's the man who makes us all. Ladies and Gentlemen, I give you Sacker-Lowell's very own Robert Merkin.

Then, Merkin.

MERKIN: Past few weeks, the news, the papers have been filled with nasty words about a pending deal all of us in this room are watching pretty closely. Saratoga-McDaniels's ongoing bid for Everson Steel. A deal, which, of course, was financed by the money many of you put up. Reading, seeing some of these pieces on the news, you'd think we were like *locusts* come upon the land. All the images of small-town life, workers coming through the gates, hard hats, lunch boxes, fathers, the *fathers* who we're told will be out of jobs if Izzy Peterman has his way. We're told that Sacker-Lowell—and yours truly—are using financial wizardry to destroy the values that made our nation great. If we're the locusts now, the frogs can't be far behind. *(Beat)* I don't agree with any of that. What's wrong in America right now—and there's definitely something wrong—has *nothing* to do with corporate debt. *(Beat)* I mean, all the fear-mongering around this deal, the waxing poetic about the death of American manufacturing—it feels to me sometimes like I've stepped into a collective delusion. The bizarre, self-serving belief that we, Americans, are somehow *better* than others. That American-made is better. Whether it's American steel or American cars, or televisions, or whatever. No evidence is offered. Just nostalgic rhetoric about what our fathers sacrificed and how great they were, and how *we*—here in this room—are endangering the legacy *they* left behind. And marry all this Norman Rockwell sentimentality to the racist tirades about slink-eyed Asians copying our stuff, and the dirty spics taking our jobs, and you have a picture of what is *actually* wrong with our country today. *(Beat)* There is a blindness out there right now. And it is *not* the blindness of those who see nothing but dollar signs. No. It's the blindness of a nation unwilling to question itself, unwilling to learn from the evidence of the marketplace. Because, see, the marketplace is telling us that our steel isn't as desirable as steel made in China. It isn't as cheap, as quickly produced, or superior in any way. The same with our cars, appliances, electronics. The Japanese? Making all these more cheaply. *And* better. That's the truth. Honda *is* a better car. That's why I drive one. But what do we hear in this country? "We're Americans. We invented the automobile. We built the greatest steel mills the world has ever known. God bless America." Let's set aside the revolting assumption that God doesn't bless other nations, or that somehow an American father's job is more important to his family than a Chinese father's one is to his. Let's just set aside those *lies*. Those *delusions*. And let's stick with the facts. Fact: They are winning. Fact: We need to understand why. Fact: We need to change. When you stay blind, you can't change. When you can't change, you die. And *that* is what is happening in this country right now.

APPLAUSE as...

—SHIFT TO:

SACKER-LOWELL.

Merkin's office. Rivera in the midst of recounting, exuberant. Peterman participates. Merkin listens.

RIVERA: I just kept at it. Everything Everson Steel threw out, I raised an objection.

PETERMAN: To the point, Bob, it was even starting to seem a little silly.

RIVERA: Except the judge kept sustaining my objections. All they had was conjecture. Hearsay.

PETERMAN: The whole thing about disclosure violations and margin requirements? They didn't have the evidence.

RIVERA *(To Peterman)*: Good thing we got rid of those documents.

PETERMAN: But there was the paper trail. With references to *Veronica.*

RIVERA: So Jackie Blount, the lawyer for their side, bites on that, won't let go. We ever need a new shark, by the way, we should keep her in mind.

PETERMAN: She starts in with the sordid tale of Everson's dad's affair with Veronica Lake. Clippings and photographs. How his parents divorced because of it.

RIVERA: I couldn't tell whether the judge was about to cry.

PETERMAN: Or if he had a hard-on behind the bench.

RIVERA: Objection, your honor. *Veronica* is a reference to Archie Comics. Betty, Veronica. Jughead.

MERKIN: Jughead?

RIVERA: Mr. Peterman's next takeover target is the publisher of Archie Comics.

MERKIN: And he believed that?

PETERMAN: I mean I've been buying everything else. Hi-fi. Mint extract.

RIVERA: Then, Bob, Cicero here asks to address the court.

PETERMAN: Your honor, what are we talking about? What we should be talking about is does it or does it not serve the shareholder's interest. That's the only question. Shareholders, sir, are the only party of moment in this matter.

MERKIN: Party of moment?

RIVERA *(To Merkin)*: You would have been proud.

PETERMAN: Last I checked, we were not living in a financial dictatorship—with boards and CEOs getting to decide whose interest is served. Management at Everson Steel is running interference to stop me from maximizing shareholder *value*. Your honor, it's illegal, and it is un-American.

—SHIFT TO:

EVERSON HEADQUARTERS.

Everson, Blount, Cizik. And Tresler, too.

TRESLER: When Max first came to me with the idea to do this deal, I thought, I don't know. Tough business. Tough climate. I don't know. But I went through the company's books, I went through your two-year plan for steel. There's something in it.

EVERSON: Finally someone agrees.

TRESLER: So, this company down in Alabama?

EVERSON: Jefferson-Tate.

TRESLER: That's done the renovations you're talking about—

EVERSON: They have the know-how. Changing the Bessemer mills into mini-mills. Electric arc. Hot stripping. That's what's been killing us. It would be a strategic partnership.

TRESLER: Right. I want you to understand something about me, Tom. I am not one of Robert Merkin's *toy soldiers*. I am not Israel Peterman. I am a real man with real money. No crummy notes, no crazy paper.

EVERSON: Crazy paper?

CIZIK: He means junk.

EVERSON: So how do you plan to finance the deal?

TRESLER: I have a group with interest in the pharmaceutical divisions. There's some ground to cover before we get there—

EVERSON: I don't understand. You want to sell pharmaceuticals?

TRESLER: Your plan's gutsy, but we need money to pull it off.

EVERSON: You want to break up the company?

TRESLER: It's the only way to make the numbers work.

EVERSON: I see.

TRESLER: This is warfare. I'm gonna have to pay in the mid-forties, per share, to top Peterman's bid.

BLOUNT: Wait—he's not allowed to talk about bid price.

TRESLER *(Coming in)*: Puhleeze. Those assholes at Sacker-Lowell are in LA breaking every rule there is to get this deal done. They drag us down into the mud, we better be ready to get our hands dirty.

BLOUNT: It's *collusion*.

TRESLER: Now why would anyone need to know?

BLOUNT: They wouldn't.

TRESLER: Because you want to keep working on Wall Street, don't you?

Everson is visibly starting to struggle with sudden emotions.

CIZIK: Tom, realistically, this is the only way to make peace with shareholders. A deal with Leo gives them a return on investment. And you've bought yourself time. Everybody gets what they want.

TRESLER: All in. That's the only way to do this.

Everson can't hold in his emotions any longer:

EVERSON: I need a moment.

He exits. All eye each other.

TRESLER: A moment for what?

Cizik exits after Everson.

—LIGHTS SHIFT TO SHOW:

HALLWAY.

Everson fights back tears.

As Cizik approaches him.

EVERSON: What was the crime, Max? Hmm?

CIZIK: Crime?

EVERSON: The company's not been doing great. I know that. But we were surviving. Inching toward the kind of change we need to be making. And now? Tresler's in there talking about selling my father's life's work to raise the money for me to buy back the business my grandfather started in the first place. We're going backward, Max. What did I do wrong?

CIZIK: Nothing, Tom. There's no crime.

EVERSON: Is this the future? Is this what we have to look forward to? Getting squeezed from every side for every last penny?

CIZIK: I hope not.

Pause.

EVERSON: Do you know Allegheny?

CIZIK: I was on a team that visited your father at the house in Pennsylvania twenty years ago. But we didn't spend more than a night there.

EVERSON: The town might as well be named Everson. Everson Street. Everson Avenue. Everson Heights. Everson Public Library. Everson High School. I mean it goes on and on. Three generations. Three generations that our family has lived off the labor of those people. They made us. *They* made us. Yeah, we've given back. But it was just the order of things.

CIZIK: You're a good man, Tom.

EVERSON: It's not about being good. It's about understanding who we are. It's not just a financial decision. I mean it is, but not just for shareholders. Shareholders are *not* more important to the company than the people who made it. *(Shifting, a sigh)* I must sound like a goddamn moron...

CIZIK: Of course not.

EVERSON: Even if you thought I did, you wouldn't tell me. *(Beat)* You trust this guy Tresler?

CIZIK: He's a straight shooter.

EVERSON: He likes to hear himself talk. Can he win this?

CIZIK: He will fight.

EVERSON: What's in it for him?

CIZIK: Two and a half percent of the total deal. At these numbers? Close to forty million dollars. And a chance to be the good guy.

Pause.

EVERSON: Okay. Let's do it.

—SHIFT TO:

PARK.

Tresler, Chen. Enjoying the evening.

TRESLER: It's not just about teaching that bastard in Los Angeles a lesson he will never forget. I wouldn't do the deal in the first place if I didn't think there was value there. There is. Done right, Everson is a good deal.

CHEN: But something's bothering you about it.

TRESLER: The owner. I mean, I knew his father. A shark. A real shark. Competitive as hell. No wallflower. The kind of guy who would humiliate you on the golf course if he could. And enjoy it.

CHEN: A fighter.

TRESLER: I have a tough time seeing the man I knew in that son of his.

They sit on a park bench.

TRESLER (CONT'D): Beautiful night, huh…

CHEN: Sure is.

TRESLER: Night that makes you happy to be alive.

Tresler smiles. Points, starting to lean in…

TRESLER (CONT'D): You see that building? The one with the staggered terraces?

CHEN: Right.

TRESLER: That's my apartment.

CHEN: Which one?

TRESLER: All of it.

CHEN: All of it?

TRESLER: Everything from that terrace all the way around… well, and…to the top.

CHEN: Wow.

TRESLER: Yeah. Hell of a place. Hell of a place.

He kisses her. She tenses up. And then relaxes into it. They keep kissing…

—LIGHTS SHIFT TO:

JUDY CHEN.

Steps forward. Addressing the audience. Coy, knowing.

CHEN: I took him back to my place even though we were right next to his. I thought it would be less confusing. *(Beat)* I'd been with enough older men to know it's not always going to be about the sex for me. *(Beat)* He was very concerned about my…—He went down on me. I don't really know what he was doing down there. He was very busy. I just kept thinking…He's confident, and that's wonderful. But is that because he has a billion dollars? Then I thought: He's pompous. That's not so wonderful. But that's also because he has a billion dollars. And his body's in good shape—for his age—but he has a trainer and a chef on staff. So that's the money, too. It was like everything I could think about him, good or bad, could be traced to his money. But *then* I thought, *he* made that money. Not everybody can do that. So maybe all these things *about* him, maybe they're *why*—I mean—*how* he made a billion dollars. Maybe it's not the money that defines him. Maybe he defines the money. That idea, that thought…It was at that point that I started to have an orgasm. God. It was a powerful orgasm.

—SHIFT TO:

MERKIN'S OFFICE.

Merkin and Rivera. Working over lunch. Rivera taking notes.

RIVERA *(Reading)*: Sacker-Lowell raises capital for companies to—

MERKIN: Not *capital*. Money is better. *Money* people understand. Capital is something, I don't know…weird. Scary.

RIVERA: Sacker-Lowell raises *money* for companies to grow.

MERKIN: *Helps* companies grow by raising them money.

RIVERA *(Noting)*: Okay.

MERKIN: Because companies that grow create wealth.

RIVERA: Wealth here, not money?

MERKIN: Money came first. Now comes wealth. One is the ladder to the other.

RIVERA: Right.

MERKIN: Companies that grow create wealth. Wealth creates jobs. Those jobs create more growth, more wealth, which sustains and nourishes. People feed families, send their kids to school. It's God's work.

RIVERA: That's a little much, Bob.

Just as Charlene appears.

CHARLENE: Your wife is here, Mr. Merkin. Should I—

MERKIN: Of course.

RIVERA: You want to go over this one more time before I send it to PR?

MERKIN: Take out "It's God's work" and send it.

Amy appears.

RIVERA: Amy.

AMY: Raúl. How are you?

RIVERA: Good, good.

AMY: How's Marisol?

MERKIN: Good God, don't ask.

AMY: Why? What happened? Is she okay?

RIVERA: Marisol's fine.

MERKIN: He got bored with her.

RIVERA: I didn't get bored with—

MERKIN: She was a keeper. Your mother loved her.

RIVERA *(To Merkin)*: And you're bringing this up, why exactly?

MERKIN: When you settle down and start a family, Raúl—it's only going to make you better. You'll see. When it happens, you'll see.

RIVERA: I'm gonna take care of this. That okay? Or do you want to run that by my mom first, too?—Bye, Amy. Good to see you.

Rivera leaves. Merkin comes over, kisses his wife.

MERKIN: What are you doing here?

Beat. Something's clearly wrong.

AMY: I stopped by Steven's office yesterday. To go over tax stuff. Saw a check from Boris Pronsky. For six and a half million. Not made out to Sacker-Lowell. Made out to you. Steven didn't know what it was for.

MERKIN: Well, he wouldn't.

AMY: Why not? He's our accountant.

MERKIN: It's just . . . —It's part of my arrangement with Boris.

AMY: Your *arrangement?*

MERKIN: Honey. What do you—

AMY: Why are you still doing this? You said—

MERKIN: I didn't say anything.

AMY: You sure as hell did.

MERKIN: I told you what you wanted to hear. So you would leave me alone about it.

AMY: So now it's okay to lie to me?

MERKIN: I need him for these deals. I need that muscle. It's just the reality.

AMY: Let's say that despite an MBA and a career of my own on the Street, I still don't understand something about getting these deals done. Maybe you do still need him in some way I just don't get. Even so. There is *no reason* to be taking his money. For God's sake, with all you're already making. Isn't it enough? What's another six and a half million?—

MERKIN: It's the only way I can keep him honest.

AMY: Are you serious?

MERKIN: If I don't make him pay me, he forgets who's in charge. I have to make him feel that pain. The pain of parting with his money. They don't teach that in business school.

AMY: You know what else they don't teach? How to cover your ass so you don't get thrown in jail. Taking that money *exposes* you. It's insider trading.

MERKIN: Goddamnit. How do you think J.P. Morgan made the kind of money he did? Rockefeller? Carnegie? They bent the rules. That's how they made their fortunes. And the world lived with it. No, the world loved it.

AMY: You're not bending the rules. You're breaking the law.

MERKIN: Laws belong to those who make the world. That's what I'm doing. I'm making the world.

AMY: What is this?

MERKIN: It's called *risk,* honey. And this is what it feels like.

—EXIT AMY, ENTER:

PETERMAN, RIVERA.

Heated…

RIVERA: Everson is definitely in bed with Leo Tresler.

PETERMAN: In bed? They've been fist-fucking for days. Your mole's not worth shit. First City called to tell me they're doing a deal.

MERKIN: First City?

PETERMAN: This morning.

MERKIN: They're trying to scare you into jumping ship here and going to them. So fucking transparent.

RIVERA: First City?

PETERMAN: Yes, Raúl.

MERKIN: They are going to pay for this.

PETERMAN: It's not just them. Lead editorial in today's *Journal* says we're going to lose this.

RIVERA: Surprise, surprise.

MERKIN: Who edits the *Journal*, Iz?

PETERMAN: What does that have to do —

MERKIN: Who edits the *Journal*?

PETERMAN: I don't know.

RIVERA: Terence Bancroft.

PETERMAN: Okay.

MERKIN: Married to Mary Hartely Bancroft.

RIVERA: Stephen Hartely's younger sister…

PETERMAN: Stephen Hartely…

MERKIN: CEO of First City.

RIVERA: The Mayflower set.

PETERMAN: Fuck. Me.

MERKIN: Their kind sticks together. We need to do the same. *(Beat)* It's time to shake this up. Change tactic.

PETERMAN: How?

MERKIN: I don't know. Something out of left field.

PETERMAN: Like what?

MERKIN: Something he's not expecting. Something he can't dismiss. *(Beat)* What does Tom Everson really want? At the end of the day?

RIVERA: Born into money.

MERKIN: Right.

RIVERA: Living in his father's shadow.

MERKIN: So the opinions of others are his only real currency.

RIVERA: If he shutters those steel mills, he's the one who killed
what his family took generations to build.

PETERMAN: Which is why he wants to keep it on its feet.

MERKIN: Whatever the consequences.

PETERMAN: Man with a death wish.

MERKIN: Fine. He wants to hang himself? Give him a noose. And
make it pretty.

—SHIFT TO:

EVERSON HEADQUARTERS.

Blount reads from the offer letter.
As Everson and Cizik listen in.

BLOUNT: Peterman agrees not to sell the steel division.

EVERSON: What?

BLOUNT: No sale of the steel division to any outside party for a
period of eight months. During which time they will negotiate its sale to you at a better-than-market price.

CIZIK: Really?

BLOUNT: There's more. Your first parachute payment is twelve
million. Your second? Eighteen. For a total of thirty million
dollars.

EVERSON: It's an insult masked as a bribe.

BLOUNT: It's the best exit package *I*'ve ever heard of.

CIZIK: Don't you see, Tom? They blinked. You've won.

EVERSON: How?

CIZIK: They're giving you the money to buy back steel.

BLOUNT: But you could pocket the thirty million and finance the purchase with debt instead. You could make *fifty, seventy* million.

EVERSON: I'm worth twice that and change as it is, Ms. Blount. I don't need more.

CIZIK *(Taking the sheet)*: Shareholders would be very happy with this—

EVERSON: Fucking shareholders.

CIZIK: And most importantly, it leaves you the room to partner with someone who sees what you see—

EVERSON: No one sees what I see. Tresler's the only one even willing to try. This is not just some business deal.

BLOUNT: Then what is it?

Everson lets out a sudden sound of frustration.

EVERSON: I don't want *Israel* Peterman anywhere near any part of this deal! He and his *friends* have done nothing but insult me and the legacy of this company from the moment this godforsaken thing started. Maybe that's how *his people* like to do business. But I will not have any part of it.

CIZIK: His people, Tom?

EVERSON: No deal with Peterman, Max. Not now. Not on Saturdays. Not ever.

Everson takes the letter from Cizik, tears it up, hands the torn letter back to Blount. Walks out.

Blount turns to Cizik:

BLOUNT: Saturdays?

CIZIK: I mean...

BLOUNT: Max. That's not right.

—QUICK SHIFT TO:

BLOUNT AND RIVERA.

On phones.

RIVERA: Did he give a reason?

BLOUNT: He called it an insult masked as a bribe.

RIVERA: He's irrational. He's leaving fifty, seventy million on the table.

BLOUNT: He's not in it for the money.

RIVERA: Silver fucking spoon. Must be nice.

BLOUNT: I'll tell you when I have my own set.

RIVERA: You and me both, Jack. You and me both.

BLOUNT: Tresler's filled his head up with talk about getting steel back on its feet.

RIVERA: It's a pipe dream.

BLOUNT: Why do you think I'm still talking to you?

RIVERA: Bob's not going to stop. He's not going to let Tresler or anybody else outbid him. It's never enough for him. That's why he's king.

BLOUNT: Raúl—

RIVERA: Tom should just let Peterman buy it. Peterman's happy to sell steel to the two of them. Then they can go off and play with steel all they want.

BLOUNT: That's not gonna happen.

RIVERA: Why not?

BLOUNT: He was very clear. He doesn't want your *boys* anywhere near the company.

RIVERA: What's that all about?

BLOUNT: Well, funny you should ask...

—QUICK SHIFT TO:

SACKER-LOWELL.

Rivera, now with Merkin and Peterman.

PETERMAN: Saturdays?

RIVERA: That's what he said.

PETERMAN: What's that even mean?

RIVERA: Who does deals on Saturdays anyway?

MERKIN: C'mon, Iz.

PETERMAN: What, Bob?

MERKIN: We've dealt with guys like this our whole lives. Guys who'd laugh at us when we tried to get a job at their banks, their firms, whatever. Shut out our dads. I mean, for God's sake, my father? Graduated top of his class, Brooklyn College. Couldn't get an *interview* at Hartford, Jordan Guaranty, half a dozen other white-shoe firms in the city he'd had his heart set on. It shouldn't have been a thing. Here's a guy. Loyal. To a fault. Sharp as a razor. Good with numbers—

RIVERA: *Staggering* with numbers.

MERKIN *(Continuing)*: Right. But who ends up going through life thinking the best he can do is disappear into the woodwork. Balance the books of dry cleaners and dentists. That's what this is about. But we're not gonna let them hold us back. We're gonna change it. Once and for all.

Charlene appears:

CHARLENE: Mr. Merkin, Boris Pronsky on line two. He says it's urgent. And Murray Lefkowitz is still holding on line three.

MERKIN *(To Charlene)*: Got it, Charlene. Thanks. *(Back to Peterman)* We are going to bury them. No matter how high we have to go.

PETERMAN: With what money, Bob?

MERKIN: I'll raise it.

PETERMAN: But I mean...

MERKIN: What?

PETERMAN: At what price does this start to—

MERKIN: You don't want it now?

PETERMAN: No, no. I do.

MERKIN: Cause if you don't, tell me. This is not just some deal.

PETERMAN: Bob.

MERKIN: I picked you. I will find someone else...

PETERMAN: No, no. I want it. I'm just saying, I'll have to run this company. This is a lot of debt.

MERKIN: You'll figure it out.

—LIGHTS OUT ON RIVERA AND PETERMAN.

—A POOL OF LIGHT SHOWS:

PRONSKY.

—ANOTHER POOL APPEARS, SHOWING:

MERKIN.

MERKIN: What's up, Boris?

PRONSKY: How are you?

MERKIN: Busy.

PRONSKY: Well, there's a problem.

MERKIN: With what?

PRONSKY: That check for the six and a half.

MERKIN: What about it? I cashed it.

PRONSKY: No, I know, I just...

MERKIN: Cough it up, for God's sake.

PRONSKY: My fucking accountant, Bob. Opened his mouth. Now they're wondering where the money's coming from.

MERKIN: Who's wondering?

PRONSKY: An audit.

MERKIN: Why is that my problem—

PRONSKY: Price Waterhouse, Bob.

MERKIN: Fine—

PRONSKY: We don't want it to be on the record—

MERKIN: I said fine.

PRONSKY: Can we call it—

MERKIN: Whatever you call it, just don't call it what it is.

PRONSKY: You think I would be that—

MERKIN: What, stupid? Sure. Why not?—

PRONSKY: Bob—

MERKIN: I don't put anything past you.

PRONSKY: Why do you have to be so mean?

MERKIN: Because you like it. *(Beat)* Charlene! Charlene!

CHARLENE: Yes, Mr. Merkin.

MERKIN: Boris Pronsky. Needs some documentation. Get him what he needs.

CHARLENE: Yes, sir. And Murray Lefkowitz is still on line three.

MERKIN: Thanks. *(Back to Pronsky)* Everson's headed higher— at least fifty-two. Keep loading up.

PRONSKY: I'm pretty overexposed on this right now, Bob—

MERKIN: Do as you're told, Boris.

PRONSKY: Fine.

MERKIN: And don't forget. Half of what you make is mine.

—SHIFT TO:

MURRAY.

Who we will recall from an early sequence in the play. He looks even more nervous now than he did then.

MERKIN: What's up, Murr?

MURRAY: Hey, Bob.

MERKIN: Yeah.

MURRAY: I, uh... —need you to buy me out.

MERKIN: Of what?

MURRAY: Bonds in Saratoga-McDaniels.

MERKIN: We're mid-deal. Izzy's putting in a new bid on Everson. Saratoga's gonna win this.

MURRAY: It's not that.

MERKIN: So what is it?

MURRAY: It's Macie, Bob.

MERKIN: Macie.

MURRAY: She's upset by what's going on, people may be losing their jobs, and—

MERKIN: Murr. I get it. Their PR is going after us. It's gonna pass.

MURRAY: Bob, I just... —It's her money.

MERKIN: You want me to talk to her? I'd be happy to help her understand.

MURRAY: No, that won't help. She thinks you're...

MERKIN: She's thinks I'm what?

MURRAY: It doesn't matter. I just... —I need the money back.

MERKIN: Okay, okay. *(Beat)* Ten cents on the dollar.

MURRAY: What?

MERKIN: I'll buy you out. Ten cents on the dollar.

MURRAY: How can you... — You promised... — You promised to buy me back if I didn't want —

MERKIN: Yes I did. I promised to buy you back. But I didn't promise you a price.

MURRAY: That's five million dollars. I gave you fifty.

MERKIN: Take it or leave it, Murr. *(Beat)* You want to talk it over with Macie?

MURRAY: You know what? She's right. You're a bully.

MERKIN: No, no, I'm your friend. And I see things you don't. Like what *you* really want.

MURRAY: I want out of the deal. I just want my money back. Like you promised.

MERKIN: Ten cents on the dollar.

MURRAY: I can't do it for that. You know I can't.

MERKIN: Now you're seeing reason.

MURRAY *(Getting emotional)*: Bob. Please.

MERKIN: Murr. This deal. Is happening. And when it does, those bonds'll be headed higher. The more you have in, the more you make.

MURRAY *(Breaking down)*: You can't do this to me. Please. Bob.

MERKIN: Murray... *(Off a long pause)* Murr, are you there?

MURRAY *(Whimpering)*: Yeah.

MERKIN: Listen to me. Just forget about your wife, forget about Macie, just for a second. Just hear me out...

—LIGHTS OUT ON MURRAY.

—AS MERKIN STEPS BACK INTO:

SACKER-LOWELL.

Joining Rivera and Peterman.

RIVERA: What did Murray want?

MERKIN: He wants to put in another twenty-five million.

RIVERA: You're kidding.

PETERMAN: In for a penny, in for a pound.

RIVERA: Deal of the decade.

MERKIN: He won't regret it.

PETERMAN: If you *can't* take money from your friends, who *can* you take it from?

—LIGHTS OUT ON SACKER-LOWELL.

—LIGHTS UP ON:

INTERROGATION ROOM.

At the US Attorney's office.

Now gathered: Addesso, Walsh, O'Hare, and counsel, Corrigan Wiley—of recognizable Irish stock.

ADDESSO *(To O'Hare)*: We have you for insider trading, manipulation of markets, tax fraud...

WALSH: Evading net capital requirements...

ADDESSO: The counts are adding up.

WILEY: My client hasn't done anything wrong.

WALSH: We beg to differ.

WILEY: Even if you had a guilty party—which you don't—you guys know you'd have a tough time winning any of those cases.

WALSH: You want to try it, be our guest.

WILEY: No, see, what I know? You *don't* want to try it. Which is why we're having this little conversation. Because you're looking to offer a deal.

WALSH: Cooperation would be appreciated, and will of course be taken into consideration—

WILEY: Cut the shit, Kevin. You're not on TV. You sound like a fucking idiot.

ADDESSO: Hey, hey, hey—

WILEY: Joe—

ADDESSO: Corry. I've got one word for you. RICO.

WILEY: Wait, what?

ADDESSO: You heard me. RICO.

WALSH: Racketeer Influenced and Corrupt Organizations—

WILEY *(Coming in)*: I know what it is, Kevin.

WALSH: For your client's benefit.

WILEY: Completely ridiculous. RICO was passed to go after the Mob. My client is not—

ADDESSO: Under RICO? All we need are two related felonies and a pattern of criminality. We've got way more than two counts of insider trading. And sure looks like we can show it's part of a pattern. Wouldn't you say, Kevin?

WALSH: Oh, I would.

WILEY: You're gonna use my client to bring the first RICO indictment on white-collar crime known to man? Am I hearing this right?

ADDESSO: He's as good a place to start as any.

WILEY: Can I have a moment, please? *(Beat)* With my client?

Once Addesso and Walsh exit:

O'HARE: What the fuck is he talking about.

WILEY: He's looking to make headlines. They're saying he wants to be mayor.

O'HARE: RICO? I'm not a mobster.

WILEY: My guess? They know about your relationship with Boris Pronsky. They're trying to scare you into giving them what they need to bring Pronsky in. That they're willing to use RICO on you? Tells me how *bad* I think they want Pronsky.

O'HARE: So you're saying…

WILEY: RICO could be a bluff. And RICO aside, they still have to make the case in front of a jury. Which isn't gonna be easy.

O'HARE: So we *don't* take a plea?

WILEY: We fight it? You win? Addesso ends up looking like a jackass.

O'HARE: And I don't have to rat out Boris…

WILEY: If it's a bluff. *(Beat)* If it *isn't* a bluff…

O'HARE: Yeah?

WILEY: Under RICO, they don't wait for a guilty verdict to seize assets. They do *that* on the day they indict.

O'HARE: Shit.

WILEY: And RICO means *triple damages,* Mark. Lets the Feds take three times what they allege you made illegally.

O'HARE: Three times?

WILEY: Before we even get to trial.

O'HARE: I don't have that, Corry. That would clean me out.

WILEY: So what I'm saying is, if this RICO stuff is *not* a bluff, you're a dead man.

—LIGHTS SHIFT TO SHOW:

TRESLER AND CIZIK.

Tresler looking concerned.

TRESLER: I don't know. I don't like how this feels. High-forties was one thing. What you're talking about—this is getting risky—

CIZIK: Peterman's new bid is going to be closer to fifty-two.

TRESLER: How do you know?

CIZIK: The market knows. Merkin's been working the phones to raise another three hundred million.

TRESLER: It's sick, Max.

CIZIK: Leo—

TRESLER: It's a sickness. Mark my words—

CIZIK: We don't have time for the lectures. We need a decision.

TRESLER: I'm telling you, low- to mid-fifties, I don't have it.

CIZIK: So we find the rest.

TRESLER: How?

CIZIK: Paper.

TRESLER: Paper. You mean junk.

CIZIK: Well, it's not gonna be triple A.

TRESLER: Max. Have you heard anything I've said? Ever? In my life?

CIZIK: I don't like loading company balance sheets with debt any better than you do. I mean, it's company balance sheets now. But you know city councils and state governments will follow. Then consumers. And then what?

TRESLER: Then we won't be a country anymore, Max. Just a business. And the only thing we'll be manufacturing? Debt.

CIZIK: Tom is still making steel, Leo. To keep doing it, he needs you.

TRESLER: With a bid into the mid-fifties…I don't know.

CIZIK: You'll be the man who saved Everson Steel. Every paper in this country will have your picture in it.

—SHIFT TO:

CIZIK AND BLOUNT.

CIZIK: We're getting close. Tresler's agreed—at least in theory—to fifty-five dollars a share.

BLOUNT: At fifty-five he has to do it with junk.

CIZIK: He knows that.

BLOUNT: He's okay with that?

CIZIK: He's in too deep. Now it's about pride.

BLOUNT: Fifty-five won't get him out of Peterman's reach.

CIZIK: Maybe I can get another dollar. But there's no way Tresler's going higher than that.

BLOUNT: Amazing. We put this deal together. Now First City comes in. Does the junk raise for him. They net seventy million.

CIZIK: Seventy million?

BLOUNT: In fees. At least.

CIZIK *(Quietly)*: My God.

BLOUNT: And we don't see a penny of that. Not a penny. Because we're not the ones raising the money.

CIZIK: We have our fee.

BLOUNT: A million, a million five if we're lucky.

CIZIK: We have to be happy with it.

BLOUNT: We're getting left behind.

CIZIK: Be that as it may.

BLOUNT: Max.

CIZIK: Whatever we're getting paid, Jackie, we have a job to do. And that job is about taking care of the client. Not trying to find new ways to gouge them for more.

BLOUNT: Banks like First City and Sacker-Lowell are leaving us in the dust. Sooner or later, you will lose your best people to those who are doing these deals.

CIZIK: Are you threatening me?

BLOUNT: Not yet.

—LIGHTS OUT ON CIZIK.

—LIGHTS UP ON:

RIVERA AND BLOUNT.

On phones.

RIVERA: Are you kidding me?

BLOUNT: And this, after Tresler's spent weeks jabbering about how much he hates junk—

RIVERA: Fucking clusterfuck.

BLOUNT: If I have to hear him talk about *crazy paper* one more time—

RIVERA: What's the bid?

BLOUNT: Fucking hypocrite.

RIVERA: Jackie, what's the bid?

BLOUNT: Fifty-five now.

RIVERA: That's fine.

BLOUNT: Maybe fifty-six later.

RIVERA: We top that, too.

BLOUNT: You may not have time.

RIVERA: What are you talking about?

BLOUNT: Max wants to call an emergency board meeting by phone.

RIVERA: For when?

BLOUNT: Tomorrow.

RIVERA: They can't do that.

BLOUNT: They can't. But they are.

RIVERA: We need to get on a plane.

BLOUNT: I'll call you as soon as I know more.

—SHIFT TO:

O'HARE.

With Walsh. And the reel-to-reel. Walsh nods at O'Hare as…

—LIGHTS UP ON:

PRONSKY.

PRONSKY: Pronsky.

O'HARE: Fuck you, Boris.

PRONSKY: Excuse me?

O'HARE: And fuck your mother.

Walsh looks concerned.
O'Hare gestures that he knows what he's doing.

PRONSKY: Mark.

O'HARE: I'm serious, Boris. I've had it with you.

PRONSKY: You need help, Mark. You've got a problem.

O'HARE: No shit I got a problem. That problem is you. And the two and a quarter percent of this dog-shit stock you've got me in.

PRONSKY: Everson Steel is not dog shit.

O'HARE: Stinking up my fucking book. Can't buy or sell a god-damn thing 'cause all my cash is tied up in this turd.

PRONSKY: You've done just fine. I've made you at least eight million.

O'HARE: This deal happening or not? Because I'm about to unload.

PRONSKY: Do not. Do that, Mark. We are holding those positions for the white whale.

O'HARE: Fuck the white whale.

PRONSKY: Mark.

O'HARE: And fuck you.

PRONSKY: White whale said Everson's headed higher. Do not sell.

O'HARE: Or what?

PRONSKY: I will drop you so far out of the network you won't know what hit you. I will *never* call you with another inside tip again.

O'Hare looks over at Walsh. Who nods. Pleased.

O'HARE: Okay.

PRONSKY: Everson is headed higher. So just get a hold of yourself. And get yourself a little help for that anger problem.

O'HARE: Will do, Lurch.

PRONSKY: Mark. I am fucking warning you.

— AND UP ON:

INTERROGATION ROOM.

Pronsky before Walsh and Addesso:

ADDESSO: Evading net capital requirements, 13-D disclosure violations—

WALSH: Manipulation of markets—

ADDESSO: Conspiracy to affect the control of corporations—

WALSH: Insider trading.

ADDESSO: You've been busy, Captain Ahab.

WALSH: Still worried about losing that leg?

ADDESSO: We will charge you under RICO. Your assets will be seized on indictment. We will seek triple damages.

WALSH: That means three hundred million dollars.

PRONSKY *(Quietly)*: Fuck.

ADDESSO: Your representation has hinted at information you have to offer. Any plea deal depends on what you do for us. Is that clear?

PRONSKY: I have two questions.

WALSH: Who is Moby Dick, Mr. Pronsky?

PRONSKY: My son's trust fund. What will happen to that?

ADDESSO: Depends on what you tell us.

PRONSKY: So he *could* keep some of his—

WALSH: Moby Dick, Mr. Pronsky.

PRONSKY: How much jail time?

ADDESSO: You play ball? The least amount that's reasonable.

WALSH: Who is Moby Dick, Mr. Pronsky?

PRONSKY: Moby Dick is Robert Merkin. Of Sacker-Lowell and Associates. America's Alchemist.

ADDESSO: You don't say.

Addesso and Walsh share a look.

—LIGHTS OUT ON PRONSKY ET AL.

—LIGHTS UP ON:

MERKIN AND PETERMAN.

Peterman standing, staring out a window. Merkin in his chair, making notes.

PETERMAN: Hell of a sunset.

MERKIN: Yes it is.

PETERMAN: Gorgeous view, Bob. Really is.

Merkin gets up. Comes over.

MERKIN: How much you think it would cost? To buy it?

PETERMAN: You mean the hotel across the street?

MERKIN: I mean everything.

PETERMAN: Everything?

MERKIN: All of it. From here to the ocean. Century City.

PETERMAN: West Los Angeles.

MERKIN: Santa Monica. Wilshire to Venice. The hills to the harbor.

PETERMAN: That's a lot of land, Bob.

MERKIN: The land. The grass. The trees. Every building. Every house. Every park. Every school. Everything.

PETERMAN: I mean…

MERKIN: If you had to guess…

PETERMAN: There's stuff you couldn't buy.

MERKIN: Like what?

PETERMAN: Post office.

MERKIN: This is America, Iz. Come on.

PETERMAN: We'd probably run the post office better anyway. *(Beat)* I don't know, Bob. No idea.

MERKIN: Take a guess.

PETERMAN: Today's prices…A few billion at least…

MERKIN: At least.

PETERMAN: Ten?

MERKIN: Maybe more. Twenty.

PETERMAN: Twenty billion. Wow. I like the sound of *that*.

Turning to Peterman.

MERKIN: Fifty. How do you like the sound of *that?*

PETERMAN: I mean...

MERKIN: A hundred.

PETERMAN: Jesus.

MERKIN: Two hundred.

PETERMAN: Bob. Is that even—

MERKIN: Possible? Of course. When you're making the world, Iz? Really making it?—You know how much John D. Rockefeller was worth when he died? Two hundred fifty billion.

PETERMAN *(Dumbfounded)*: Two hundred fifty billion dollars.

MERKIN: But I don't even know if that's the number.

PETERMAN: For what?

MERKIN: To feel—I don't know. Like it's...*enough.*

PETERMAN: C'mon, Bob. You don't know the meaning of the word.

MERKIN: It's not greed, Iz.

PETERMAN: I know. It's what makes you great. But you gotta be careful. My dad always says: When you don't define your own limit, the limit comes to find you.

MERKIN: *(After a beat)* How much's your dad worth?

PETERMAN: Twenty-five million. It's enough for him.

MERKIN: That enough for you?

PETERMAN: Fuck no.

—SHIFT TO:

EVERSON.

On a late-night phone call with Cizik. Everson clutches a tumbler filled with ice and scotch. Cizik is in a cashmere robe.

EVERSON: When did you speak to him last?

CIZIK: A few hours ago. He was cranky. But committed.

EVERSON: This is going to come together, right?

CIZIK: There's no reason to think it won't.

EVERSON: I mean, Tresler can't pull out now—

CIZIK: I don't see that happening. He prides himself too much on closing.

EVERSON *(Beat)*: God almighty. I'm scared, Max.

CIZIK: Try to get some rest.

EVERSON: I just—I keep thinking about Dad. What he'd do, what he'd make of this, what he'd make of me.

CIZIK: Your father would be proud.

EVERSON: I doubt that. *(Beat)* How's Matthew?

CIZIK: He's fine. Thank you for asking.

EVERSON: The new place?

CIZIK: We love it.

EVERSON: That's good.

CIZIK: I'm here if you need me.

EVERSON: Max. Thank you. For everything.

CIZIK: It's my job, Tom. Good night.

Everson stares into his drink. Then looks up to heaven.

EVERSON: I know I never turn to you until I have to. Forgive my selfishness. Let me win this. Let me prove myself worthy, Heavenly Father. That's all I ask. The chance to prove myself. To him. And you.

—SHIFT TO:

CHEN'S APARTMENT.

Night. Chen and Tresler in each other's arms.

TRESLER: What time is it?

CHEN: Three thirty.

TRESLER: Fuck.

CHEN: Forget about it.

TRESLER: I can't. Six and a half hours until the board vote.

CHEN: Until you can celebrate being the new owner of Everson Steel.

TRESLER: I feel like I should be read my last rites.

CHEN: Cold feet?

TRESLER: It's not cold feet. It's dread. I don't like how this is coming together. I have this gnawing feeling I've let myself be talked into this.

CHEN: You don't have to do it.

TRESLER: Somebody does. Otherwise, these guys get the message that they can do whatever they want. And I do not want to live in that world.

CHEN: You doing this deal is not going to stop them. If they don't get Everson, they'll try something else. Merkin is a true believer.

TRESLER: Yeah, well, Rasputin was a true believer.

CHEN: Merkin is hardly Rasputin.

TRESLER: You're not gonna tell me you've bought into that whole dog and pony show, too?

CHEN: No. I'm just saying—

TRESLER: You said you thought he was a liar—

CHEN: He's definitely hiding things behind all that talk of

revolution…—You know what I found out? He's not just lending money. His bonds come with guarantees of ownership that he doesn't disclose to anyone. He keeps them for himself.

TRESLER: Taking his pound of flesh.

CHEN: He basically ends up owning almost every company he finances. Nobody knows it.

TRESLER: You putting *that* in your book?

CHEN: Yes.

TRESLER: He's a pawnbroker. And he's got America in hock.

CHEN: Or he's the new J.P. Morgan.

Beat.

TRESLER: Maybe you want to be with him right now.

CHEN: What are you talking about?

TRESLER: I don't know. Sounds like maybe you'd rather be with him right now.

CHEN: You're talking crazy.

TRESLER: Maybe not.

CHEN: Stop, Leo. That's not funny.

TRESLER: I'm not trying to be funny.

CHEN: Come here. Stop talking crazy.

She draws him close. They kiss.

CHEN (CONT'D): That better?

She kisses him again. They proceed. Until Tresler stops her:

TRESLER: Is that in your book?

CHEN: What?

TRESLER: The J.P. Morgan thing.

CHEN: I mean…

TRESLER: It is.

CHEN: It's a comparison I make at one point.

Pause. Tresler gets up. Grabs his clothes.

CHEN (CONT'D): What are you doing?
TRESLER: I think I should go.
CHEN: It's three thirty in the morning.

Tresler dresses in silence.

CHEN (CONT'D): Leo. Leo.
TRESLER: What?
CHEN: God, what is it with you and Robert Merkin?

Suddenly:

TRESLER: A man is a funny thing, Judy. A man *is* what he *has.* That's the truth. Nobody wants to admit it. Everybody wants to say it's something else. Something more noble. But it's not. What a man *has* is what makes him in the eyes of the world, and in his own eyes. *(Beat)* And the last thing a man wants to feel is that there's another man out there who has what he doesn't, and that the woman he might be falling in love with knows it.
CHEN: Leo.
TRESLER: I gotta go.

Tresler exits.

—SHIFT TO:

THE "BOARD" MEETING.

Everson, Blount, Cizik.

And Tresler. Board Members— "B.M."—assembled over speakerphone.

Scene comes up as Cizik is reading roll call.

CIZIK: Francis D. Fergusson.

MALE B.M: Here.

CIZIK: Michael Brook.

MALE B.M.: Here.

CIZIK: Hailey Welton Perkins.

FEMALE B.M.: Here.

CIZIK: Lewis Stevens.

MALE B.M.: Here.

CIZIK: Jeffrey Y. Martin.

MALE B.M.: Here.

CIZIK: William Pollard the Third.

MALE B.M.: Here.

CIZIK: Remy Vaucluse.

MALE B.M.: Here.

CIZIK: James P. Jordan.

MALE B.M.: Here.

CIZIK: Fernanda Sutton.

FEMALE B.M.: Here.

CIZIK: Ira Charles Bernstein.

MALE B.M.: Here.

CIZIK: That's roll. Let's get started.

BLOUNT: But it's not ten o'clock yet.

CIZIK: Just a few minutes.

BLOUNT: Max.

CIZIK: We'll wait on the actual vote.

TRESLER: What are we waiting for?

EVERSON: The rules. We don't want it to seem like—

TRESLER: Like what? Like we're trying to get a deal done?

BLOUNT: We don't want to show intent to break the rules.

TRESLER: Jesus Christ. Go on.

BLOUNT: You don't want a court to vacate the decision.

TRESLER: Tom, will you get this show on the road already?

Everson turns to Cizik. Who nods.

CIZIK: Go ahead, say a few words to get things started. We'll wait until after ten for the vote.

EVERSON *(To the Board)*: Hi all, it's Tom.

We hear various Board Member voices.

EVERSON (CONT'D): I want to welcome you and thank you for making time at such short notice.

A few more responses from Board Member voices.

Blount checks her watch. Getting nervous.

EVERSON (CONT'D): The decision before you today is as significant as any that's been asked of an Everson board. You have the best interests of shareholders to consider—but I urge you to recognize, as well, the best interests of the company itself. The person who purchased Everson stock yesterday should not stand on equal footing with those who've spent their lives with our company. Please. Don't be fooled by those, who, while claiming to be invested in *our* well-being, are only interested in their own. *(Beat)* Jackie Blount of Lausanne & Company is going to read you the two bids...

BLOUNT: Israel Peterman at Saratoga-McDaniels has bid fifty-two dollars a share. A tender to be financed by Robert Merkin at

Sacker-Lowell and Associates. The second bid is Leo Tresler's for fifty-six dollars a share—

TRESLER *(Quietly, under)*: Fuck me.

BLOUNT: To be financed with a bond issue underwritten by First City Bank.

MALE B.M. *(Coming in)*: Doesn't sound like much of a decision, Tom. Don't know what the hullaballoo is all about. Four-dollar difference?

Laughs.

EVERSON: Lewis, I think that's you...

MALE B.M.: Yes, it is.

EVERSON: Well, we're legally bound to consider all bids.

MALE B.M.: Okay, well, my niece just told me she'd bid a dollar.

Suddenly broken by a commotion at the door. Robert Merkin and Raúl Rivera come into the room. Cizik in tow.

MERKIN *(Over, announcing)*: It is not ten o'clock! The official deadline for the period of bidding has not ended!

RIVERA: A deadline—I might add—that was *not* made public to Saratoga-McDaniels...

MALE B.M: Who is that?

MERKIN: Bob Merkin. Sacker-Lowell—

RIVERA: Raúl Rivera. Legal at Sacker-Lowell—

TRESLER *(Under)*: Rivera?

RIVERA: And we're here to officially deliver Israel Peterman's revised bid for sixty-one dollars a share.

Noises erupt from the board.

TRESLER: Five fucking dollars more?!

RIVERA *(Pointing to Tresler)*: What's he doing in here?

TRESLER: Five fucking dollars!

RIVERA: He's the bidder. He's not supposed to be in here.

CIZIK: For the vote. He just can't be here for the actual vote—

RIVERA: You guys are playing dirty.

CIZIK: We haven't voted yet.

TRESLER: *We're* playing dirty? We're fucking playing dirty!

RIVERA: Language, sir.

MERKIN: Only thing illegal here is you fast-tracking this meeting—

TRESLER: Fucking shitshow!

MERKIN: —to cut us out of the process!

Moving to Merkin and Rivera, aggressive.

TRESLER: I've got half a mind to—

CIZIK: Leo!

RIVERA: To what? To do what?

TRESLER: Lay you out! You fucking *spic*—

CIZIK: Leo! Stop it!

The Board erupts.

RIVERA: Put a leash on this guy—

MERKIN: That's how you Princeton boys handle things, isn't it? Slurs and fists? How's that working out for you?

Cizik is in the middle now. Pushing Tresler back.

CIZIK: Leo, calm down! Calm down!

Merkin turns his attention to the board.

MERKIN: Ladies and Gentlemen of the board, this bid of sixty-one dollars a share—

TRESLER: Crummy notes! Crazy paper!

RIVERA: Your bid's a junk tender, too.

TRESLER: Don't you talk to me!

RIVERA: Just *our* junk is a thousand times more viable than anything you can put—

TRESLER: Viable!? Viable!?—

MALE B.M.: You need to calm down, Leo.

TRESLER: What do these people even mean when they speak anymore?!

ANOTHER B.M.: We need to hear more about this new bid.

TRESLER: You gonna let them get away with this?

EVERSON: Would you please calm down? We'll handle this.

TRESLER *(Beat)*: You know what? You'll handle it without me. That's it. I'm through.

CIZIK: What are you talking about?

TRESLER: I can't do this. I haven't felt good about it.

EVERSON: You're just going to *walk away?*

TRESLER: I can't bury your father's great company with all this debt.

EVERSON: My father's company?

TRESLER: I can't be a party to it. And I won't be.

EVERSON: My father knew how to do more than just talk, Mr. Tresler.

TRESLER *(Turning to the board)*: I officially retract my bid. I apologize to the board. I wish you all the best.

A chaotic din breaks out in the room. Tresler heads for the exit...

CIZIK: Where are you going?

TRESLER: They're not just at the gates, Max. They're coming in over the wall. And they're coming for you next.

Tresler exits.

EVERSON: Do I have a motion to adjourn this meeting?

RIVERA: You can't adjourn! You have to take a vote on our bid!

MERKIN: Ladies and Gentlemen —

MALE B.M.: Move to adjourn.

RIVERA: You second that motion and we will sue you!

EVERSON: Do I have a second?

MERKIN *(Emphatic)*: Tom. You can't do this. You know you can't —

RIVERA *(Shouting)*: We will sue you! —

EVERSON: Do I have a second, people? —

RIVERA: For breach of process!

FEMALE B.M.: Wait, Tom. We need to discuss this.

MALE B.M.: Hailey's right.

EVERSON: Right about what?

MALE B.M.: We need to talk about this.

RIVERA: You have to vote on our bid!

MALE B.M.: If there isn't another bid, we need to talk about this one.

RIVERA: You are legally. Obligated.

MERKIN: Ladies and Gentlemen —

EVERSON: People. If I don't have a second for this motion . . .

MALE B.M.: Tom —

FEMALE B.M.: There isn't going to be a second.

MALE B.M.: We need to discuss this.

EVERSON: What are we discussing?

MERKIN: Breach of your bound duty to shareholders —

EVERSON: Bound duty?

MERKIN: —fiduciary oversight of shareholder —

EVERSON: What about my bound duty as a *citizen*?

MERKIN: Every person on this board is paid a salary, Mr. Everson—

RIVERA: Most of them upwards of two hundred thousand dollars, might I add—

EVERSON *(Over)*: What about my *bound duty* to the people who built this company?—

MERKIN: And you are paying these board members to perform a duty. To increase this company's financial value.

RIVERA: Anything else, Mr. Everson, is rank sentimentality—

FEMALE B.M.: He's not wrong, Tom.

EVERSON: We didn't ask for a buyout! We didn't want one! We didn't need one, not until these people came along!

RIVERA: And that's relevant *how?*

MERKIN: Mr. Peterman's bid increases this company's value by nearly three quarters of a billion dollars over any other bid.

MALE B.M.: That is a lot of money.

EVERSON *(Struggling)*: Three quarters of a billion dollars more in *debt.* On top of the rest of the debt we've already...— none of which the company can afford. It'll choke our finances...Pull apart what it took a hundred years to put together. If that's your idea of—increasing *value...*

Everson is overcome with emotion. Merkin comes in:

MERKIN: Ladies and gentlemen of the board. We are here to save Everson Steel from death and decay. This bid is an invitation to change. To grow. To find new life. New life in the marketplace.

FEMALE B.M.: It would be very difficult to justify not taking a bid like this.

MALE B.M.: Shareholders would be doing very well at sixty-one.

ANOTHER B.M.: Yes they would.

MALE B.M.: It's ten o'clock.

Pause.

ANOTHER B.M.: Do we have a motion for a vote?
MALE B.M.: So moved.
ANOTHER B.M.: I second.
MALE B.M.: All in favor?
EVERSON: Please. Don't.
MALE B.M.: All in favor?

Beat.

ALL BOARD MEMBERS: Aye.
MALE B.M.: Opposed.

Silence.

MALE B.M. (CONT'D): Ayes have it.
EVERSON: Congratulations.

—LIGHTS OUT.

—A POOL OF LIGHT ON:

MERKIN.

The sound of a phone ringing.

—ANOTHER POOL OF LIGHT ON:

PETERMAN.

PETERMAN: Peterman.

MERKIN: Izzy, it's Bob.

PETERMAN: Bob.

MERKIN: We got it.

PETERMAN: We got it?!

MERKIN: Sixty-one a share.

PETERMAN: Unfuckingbelievable!

MERKIN: You are the new owner of Everson Steel.

PETERMAN: Oh…my…God…How was it?

MERKIN: Bit of a shit show, to quote Tresler.

PETERMAN: He was there?

MERKIN: Of course he was. We all got into it.

PETERMAN: Let's meet up. Get everyone together at the Russian Tea Room. Pop some bubbly.

MERKIN: You go. Have fun. I'm headed to the airport. Getting the next flight out.

Beat.

PETERMAN: Bob…Thank you.

MERKIN: All eyes are on you now, Izzy. This is the big time. Do right by it. Make us all proud.

PETERMAN: I will. I will.

—LIGHTS OUT ON PETERMAN.

—A POOL OF LIGHT UP ON:

PRONSKY.

With Walsh, who has headphones on. And Addesso.

MERKIN: Boris.

PRONSKY: Bob?

MERKIN: Everson went through.

PRONSKY: That's great, Bob.

MERKIN: No, I mean the bid. Sixty-one. There's a window. Two hours before it gets announced.

PRONSKY: Okay?

MERKIN: Boris?

PRONSKY: What?

MERKIN: Do I have to spell this out for you? It's trading at fifty-six. You've got two hours to load up before it jumps.

PRONSKY: Sixty-one?

MERKIN: That's what I said.

PRONSKY: You want me to buy it now, because you know that it's going to sixty-one?

MERKIN: Are you on something right now?

PRONSKY: No. I mean...No.

MERKIN: I just walked out of the board meeting. Sixty-one. Get in now. You have two hours.

PRONSKY: Okay.

MERKIN: And don't forget. Half of every penny you make is mine. Good-bye.

—LIGHTS OUT ON MERKIN.

Pronsky hangs up. Looks at Walsh.
Walsh turns to Addesso. With a nod.

—LIGHTS OUT ON PRONSKY ET AL.

—AS WE SEE:

TOM EVERSON.

Far upstage. Pacing back and forth.
Absorbed. Distraught.

—AND TWO POOLS OF LIGHT SHOW:

MERKIN AND MURRAY.

Sounds of an airport. At first, nondescript. Then more distinct.

MURRAY: Hello?

MERKIN: Murr. It's Bob.

MURRAY: Bob.

MERKIN: Just wanted you to know. You and Macie. The deal went through.

MURRAY: It did?

MERKIN: And you are going to make a nice tidy sum, Murr. Thanks for coming in. Thanks for sitting tight.

Murray is quiet. Feeling emotional.

MERKIN (CONT'D): Murr? You there?

MURRAY: Yeah, Bob. I am.

MERKIN: Just wanted you to know. Didn't want you to worry.

MURRAY: I'm sorry, Bob. About the things I said. For not trusting you.

MERKIN: It's okay. It happens. All's well that ends well.

MURRAY: I love you, Bob.

MERKIN: Love you, too, Murr. Give my best to Macie.

—LIGHTS OUT ON MURRAY.

—LIGHTS UP ON:

WALSH.

Sidling up to Merkin.

WALSH: Robert Merkin?
MERKIN: Yes.
WALSH: Of the investment bank Sacker-Lowell and Associates?
MERKIN: The same.
WALSH: Kevin Walsh, US Attorney's office.
MERKIN: Can I help you?
WALSH: I believe you can.

Walsh leads him off.

—AND:

TOM EVERSON.

Pulls out a gun. And shoots himself.

END OF ACT TWO.

Act Three

SIX MONTHS LATER

STEELWORKERS UNION HALL.

Workers at the Everson Steel Mill, in hard hats and work fatigues. Gathered before a platform, where a UNION REP stands, holding a piece of paper.

UNION REP: Have to be honest. I'm disgusted with you. Pretty much all of you, according to the vote. Six months ago we buried Tom Everson. In his will, he left all of you ninety percent of his family holdings in the company. I get up here three weeks ago, and map out how we can use that money to benefit all of you, together. I told you all you'd see more money over the next fifteen years if you voted on a union-managed annuity rather than taking the cash now—and that would have helped keep the union strong. D'ya listen? Not a chance. *(Reading)* Ninety percent. Split up between you—comes out to three hundred and forty-two shares per employee. Just south of twenty-one thousand dollars to each of you. Barely half a full year's wages for most. Shortsighted. Stupid. And the vote wasn't even close. *(Off the paper)* Thirteen thousand to three hundred.

Murmurs and demonstrations of satisfaction erupt, rippling through the crowd.

UNION REP (CONT'D): All I can say is invest the money wisely. Not sure you'll have these jobs that much longer. God help you all.

—SHIFT TO:

NEW YORK HOTEL ROOM.

Merkin, Amy, Counsel. Counsel reads from an indictment report open before him. Merkin paces. Amy is tense, haggard.

COUNSEL: These seventeen counts...

AMY: Seventeen.

COUNSEL: All variations on failure to disclose. We can make a case that these are not on him...

AMY: They're not. Accounting. Standards and practices.

COUNSEL: Legal.

AMY: Right. Legal.

MERKIN: No.

AMY: What?

MERKIN: I'm not throwing Raúl under the bus.

AMY: Who said anything about throwing—

MERKIN: You said legal. Raúl is legal at Sacker-Lowell.

AMY: He's not the one being prosecuted, Bob. You are. Blaming legal doesn't have the same ramifications.

MERKIN: I am not throwing him under the bus. He's on our side. I need him.

Amy turns away.

COUNSEL: Fine. Put it on reporting, accounting. *(Back to the report)* Thirteen counts of net capital violations.

AMY: He can reasonably plead ignorance.

MERKIN: Which doesn't absolve me in the eyes of the law.

COUNSEL: But the jury might believe you didn't know...

AMY: He didn't.

COUNSEL: So, that's seventeen. Plus the thirteen from before. Thirty.

AMY: Thirty. Thirty counts we can beat.

COUNSEL: Going on...Fourteen counts of misrepresentation of securities, defrauding of clients, conspiracy to commit these acts.

AMY: None of his clients felt defrauded. He made them all money.

COUNSEL: So they testify.

AMY: Character witnesses will be stellar.

MERKIN: People are not returning our calls.

AMY: When they know you're going to fight this, they will.

COUNSEL: With solid character witnesses, I think the jury sides with you on those.

AMY: So that's fourteen, plus the thirty.

COUNSEL: Forty-four. *(Turning a page)* Which still leaves fifty-two.

AMY: Jesus.

MERKIN: And those...?

AMY *(Finishing, impetuous)*: Are the record of your disgusting passion for that creep.

Tense pause.

COUNSEL: Look. Pronsky lies for a living, buying and selling on rumor. They look at him? They look at you? There is a very good chance they side with you.

AMY: He's right.

MERKIN: Giving that money to his employees made Tom Everson a saint. When I'm up on that stand, they will do everything they can to paint me as the man who killed a saint.

AMY: And *we* will paint him as a man too weak for the world. Which is what he was.

MERKIN: Whatever he was, he won. I didn't.

Pause.

COUNSEL *(Back to the report)*: Fifty-two. Fifty-two counts that tie you to Pronsky. That's where the trial will be played out. Fifty-two felony counts. Each with a maximum sentence of between five and ten years. For a total of three hundred eighty years of possible jail time.

MERKIN: Why don't they just hang me while they're at it?

COUNSEL: Addesso wants your head.

AMY: He wants headlines.

MERKIN: It's a goddamn witch hunt.

AMY: And you gave them exactly what they needed to make it happen.

Pause. Merkin turns to Counsel.

MERKIN: Barry. Can you give us a moment?

COUNSEL: Sure.

Counsel exits. Then:

AMY: Bob. You can win this. Get out there, tell them what you've done. Remind them: You opened faucets that were rusted shut for generations. What poured out was wealth. And not just for you. Not even mainly for you. America is back. Everybody knows it. They feel it. Remind them how much of that is because of you. We have the resources. We will craft the message. We will make them see what we want them to see. People think what they're told to think. You know that better than anyone.

MERKIN: You heard our lawyer. Addesso wants blood. He's not bluffing with the RICO indictment—

AMY: Do *not* let that man tell your story. Climbing all over you to get into the mayor's office. Expose him. Open their eyes. That guy is not looking out for anybody but himself. You've done more good for this country than Addesso ever will. *(Beat)* Bob. I will not walk through the rest of my life hanging my head in disgrace. You need to fight.

MERKIN: If we lose, we lose everything.

AMY: Maybe *that's* a risk actually worth taking.

Pause.

MERKIN: I can't. I can't do it. I can't take that chance.

AMY: Bob.

MERKIN: In this country, there's less disgrace in admitting guilt than going broke. They want to destroy me, take everything. At least if I agree to the plea—

AMY: No.

MERKIN: At least, we keep the money.

AMY: I'm fighting to save *you*. And you're fighting to save the money?

MERKIN *(Getting emotional)*: Taking the plea... Once I get out...

AMY: No.

MERKIN *(More emotional)*: We can start again...

AMY: No.

MERKIN *(Overwhelmed)*: Honey. I have to take the plea.

AMY: No.

—SHIFT TO:

PARK BENCH.

Addesso and Walsh. In overcoats. Addesso finishing a cigarette. Crushes it underfoot.

WALSH: Where is he?

ADDESSO: He's gonna make me wait. Just a little. He has to.

WALSH: I still don't understand.

ADDESSO: Kevin.

WALSH: It's very unusual.

ADDESSO: Who needs to know?

WALSH: He'll know.

ADDESSO: I don't want to try it, okay? You don't want to try it. If meeting with him gets us closer to a settlement…

WALSH: I do want to try it.

ADDESSO: I've got the mayor's race coming up, Kevin. I don't want to have a split focus. I want to get this done.

WALSH: You want headlines, Joe.

ADDESSO: Okay. I want the headlines. Crucify me.

WALSH: I'm just saying…

ADDESSO: What? What are you saying? By settling this thing without a trial, we save taxpayers, what, two, three million dollars? We get that much closer that much sooner to sending the message we want to miscreants on Wall Street. It's the greater good.

WALSH: Two years is chump change for this guy.

ADDESSO: It's a start. And it's a good start. It puts them all on notice.

WALSH: Or sends the message that you can completely game the system and line your pockets and the worst we'll do is slap you on the wrist.

Upstage, in the half-light, Merkin appears.

ADDESSO *(Turning to)*: Mr. Merkin.
MERKIN: Mr. Addesso.
ADDESSO: My associate Kevin Walsh.
MERKIN: We've met.
ADDESSO: Who will be leaving us. *(Turning)* Thanks, Kevin.

Walsh exits.

MERKIN: Thanks for meeting me.
ADDESSO: It is unusual.
MERKIN: I know. I appreciate it.
ADDESSO: What's on your mind?

Pause.

MERKIN: Where to next?
ADDESSO: Excuse me?
MERKIN: After Gracie Mansion, I mean. Assuming you win. What comes next? Senate? Or straight to the White House?
ADDESSO: Maybe concern yourself a little bit less with my future and a little more with your own.
MERKIN: Right. If you end up in the White House some ten, fifteen years from now—and who knows, you might, with the right friends...My guess is you'll come to understand all of this a little differently.
ADDESSO: And how is that?

MERKIN: Money. It's what will get you into office, *if* you get there. It's what you will lose sleep over, while you *are* there.

ADDESSO: Thank you for the tutorial—

MERKIN: Raising money. *That's* what you'll spend your time doing. And that, Mr. Addesso, is all I was really doing. Raising money.

ADDESSO: You broke the rules. Many times over.

MERKIN: So did the Continental Army. We tend to look pretty favorably on them at this point.

Addesso laughs.

ADDESSO: Didn't take you for a romantic.

MERKIN: You don't know me. *(Beat)* Five hundred million.

ADDESSO: Excuse me?

MERKIN: To plea. I'm not paying you more than five hundred million. That's what your headline'll cost you.

ADDESSO: You're in no position to negotiate.

MERKIN: The fact that you're here tells me otherwise.

Pause.

ADDESSO: You take the two counts.

MERKIN: Fine.

ADDESSO: You admit guilt.

MERKIN: Fine.

ADDESSO: And you pay nine hundred million.

MERKIN: Six.

ADDESSO: Eight.

MERKIN: Seven.

ADDESSO: Seven fifty.

Pause.

MERKIN: Fine.

ADDESSO: You sign it today.

MERKIN: We have a deal.

> *He reaches out to shake. Addesso reciprocates.*

—LIGHTS OUT ON ADDESSO AND MERKIN.

—A SPOTLIGHT DOWNSTAGE ON:

PETERMAN.

> *Looking out at the audience—as if at a mirror.*
> *Getting himself dressed in black tie. Cuff links.*

—AS LIGHTS COME UP ELSEWHERE TO SHOW:

EVERSON HEADQUARTERS.

> *Rivera, Cizik, Blount. On a conference call with Peterman.*
>
> *Both battling sides now all working together. The "New Everson"—a multiracial, multicultural synthesis with single-minded devotion to the bottom line.*
>
> *Peterman participates as he dresses. The advisers at "New Everson" speak back to him through a conference phone.*
>
> *(Perhaps there are "Assistants" coming and going with boxes of papers to contribute to the impression of activity.)*

BLOUNT: BioScan's the only pharmaceutical in the division not making money.

RIVERA: But the bio samples are a gold mine, right?

CIZIK: Largest inventory in the world. Held in deep freeze.

BLOUNT: Significant value there.

PETERMAN: What's the number?

BLOUNT: Could be as high as seventy million.

PETERMAN: Great. We need every penny we can get.

CIZIK: The debt is choking the balance sheet.

PETERMAN: And you know how you eat an elephant, Max? One bite at a time. There a buyer?

CIZIK: Two Swiss pharmaceuticals have been making overtures.

PETERMAN: How many employees at the sample company?

BLOUNT: Nine hundred.

PETERMAN: Even nine hundred people losing their jobs is front page news when I'm doing the firing. Get it done. But keep it quiet—What else?

BLOUNT: We're still working out a situation with steel.

RIVERA: There might be a bidder.

PETERMAN: *Might* be?

CIZIK: Chinese-Mexican group. But it won't be a good number.

RIVERA: Fire-sale price.

PETERMAN: The steel division is hemorrhaging money. Allegheny, Pennsylvania, is a pain in my ass. I don't want to be making steel. I don't want to be making anything. I just want to be making money.

RIVERA: Nothing makes money like money.

PETERMAN: Make it happen, Max.

CIZIK: There's no offer yet.

PETERMAN: Get one. *(Beat)* What else?

RIVERA: Reliance. Jackie went through the books.

BLOUNT: It's got a tax-loss carry-forward that runs into the hundred million dollar terrain.

PETERMAN: How complicated is it to strip the assets?

RIVERA: Not complicated. You set up a shell. Just procedure.

PETERMAN: Perfect vehicle for the next takeover.

CIZIK: Which is?

PETERMAN: Pepsi. *(Beat)* Yep. You heard me. Great product. They are going to put Coke out of business.

RIVERA: With the cash they're throwing off? You could raise more money on junk than you'd know what to do with.

PETERMAN: I'd know what to do with it.

RIVERA: Keep the acquisition price somewhere in the mid-eighties, you get the company basically for peanuts. But you need to move on it.

PETERMAN: With Bob gone, who does the raise?

CIZIK: Well—we'd be interested in talking about that. Jackie will be heading up a new department at Lausanne.

BLOUNT: Head of Debt Financing.

RIVERA: Congrats, Jackie.

BLOUNT: Thanks, Raúl.

PETERMAN: But you guys have never raised money on junk.

CIZIK: We were hoping Raúl would be willing to consult...

PETERMAN *(To Rivera)*: Raúl? Would Bob mind, I mean if you...?

RIVERA: Why would he?

PETERMAN: You're right. A fucking mensch. How's he doing?

RIVERA: All things considered...

PETERMAN: I still think he should've fought it.

RIVERA: It's just two years. And he gave up seven hundred fifty million. He walks away with three times that?

BLOUNT *(Impressed)*: Two years in prison. And he walks away with two billion dollars.

CIZIK: Nothing to aspire to.

BLOUNT: Sign me up, Max. Any time.

PETERMAN: He and Amy, though, huh?

RIVERA: She took it hard.

PETERMAN: They're not still talking about divorce, are they?

RIVERA: Not talk anymore, Iz. It's happening.

PETERMAN: And the kid. Fuck. That's tough. *(Beat)* I've got a date. Thanks, everybody.

—LIGHTS OUT ON NEW EVERSON.

—LIGHTS UP ON:

GOP FUNDRAISER.

Addesso in black tie, receiving the arrivals…

Next up, Peterman. Who approaches, leans in to say a few words to Addesso as they shake.

The conversation drowned out by the sounds of the party.

Addesso smiles as he listens. Nods.

Then responds. A conversation starting up.

As both of them turn to go inside and get a drink.

—SHIFT TO:

TRESLER.

At his office. With a GHOST WRITER (28)—white, female, attractive. She takes notes as Tresler speaks.

TRESLER: Their parents or their grandparents get off a boat, swim across a river, I don't know—they get here, start their lives—and they look out for their own. I don't blame them. I'd do the same if I was in their shoes. My loyalties would be divided. *(Beat)* I have this Pakistani doctor still sends most of his money *back home,* is what he calls it. This is still not home for him. Not really. I mean they're all thinking about some *other place* first. What's going on in Cuba? Israel... China.—The only place I'm thinking about? *This* one. The USA. But see these people come here and think opportunity means elbowing their way to the front of the line. Using the system to figure out how to make it for *their* group, *their* tribe, *their* special corner of the world. Until they've been here three, four, five generations—until they've stopped feeling like they belong to some *other place, then* we can start talking about their *investment* in this one. I mean, we can't be expected to leave the legacy of what it's taken us generations and generations to build, to leave it to—

GHOST WRITER: Us, Mr. Tresler?

TRESLER: Excuse me?

GHOST WRITER: You said *us.* Did you mean—?

TRESLER: You know, like you and me.

GHOST WRITER: You mean white.

TRESLER: I mean, I don't think you want me to say it like that.

GHOST WRITER: It's your book, Mr. Tresler. However you want to say it is how—

TRESLER: Find a different way to have me say it. A better way. That's what I'm paying you for.

GHOST WRITER: Right.

TRESLER: Like I was saying, we didn't become the greatest country in the world by having every damn group looking out for themselves. Until these people really feel like Americans and

Americans only, until they really *feel* like they belong, it's up to those of us who really *do* belong to make sure this blessed ship doesn't sink.

—SHIFT TO:

A ROOM.

Rivera. Judy Chen. And her lawyer.
Chen is going through a bound manuscript, liberally flagged.
The same manuscript before Rivera, flagged and open as well.

CHEN: And what's wrong with that sentence?

RIVERA: It wasn't an affidavit. It was a written affirmation.

CHEN: Which is different, how?

RIVERA: Bob attested to his belief there had been no willful destruction of documents. But of course, he couldn't know for certain. So we advised him not to attest to any *facts*, but simply to share, in good faith—and in an official capacity— his *opinion* that no documents were destroyed.

CHEN: His assistant attested to the contrary.

RIVERA: My point is—since it was just Bob's *opinion*, there is no issue of perjury involved. That's the other word we want removed. Perjury.

CHEN: Right.

Pause.

LAWYER: Should we move on…

Chen turns the page.

CHEN: As far as this chapter goes…

RIVERA: Chapter 10. Unacceptable. I mean there are a few paragraphs toward the close we can live with.

CHEN: A few paragraphs toward the close?

RIVERA: But the entire account alleging that Bob hid personal ownership in the companies whose takeovers he was financing?

CHEN: Is fully documented.

RIVERA: Hearsay.

CHEN: Not according to the paper trail I found. Maybe you didn't destroy enough documents.

RIVERA: Ms. Chen.

CHEN: Your boss raised money by underwriting bonds that could be converted to stock. The people entitled to that promise of equity should have been the people who bought those bonds. But they never even knew. Because he lied to his clients and pocketed the equity himself. Whether or not it's illegal, it's certainly unethical.

LAWYER: I'm sure Judy would be happy to add the word *allege* to the third sentence on page one ninety-eight. To soften —

RIVERA: Unacceptable. We can't live with any mention at all. Alleged or otherwise.

CHEN: You want me to take out the entire chapter?

RIVERA: That sounds like a great idea.

CHEN: Absolutely not.

Pause.

LAWYER: Do you mind if I ask why this is so important to you? Perhaps if we have a better understanding —

CHEN *(Coming in)*: It's because they're so married to this idea Merkin was a force for good. He really believes all that. Still. In prison.

RIVERA: Because it's true.

CHEN: I'm not changing a word. And I'm not taking it out. That or any other chapter.

RIVERA: We will press this. We will sue you for libel.

LAWYER: Libel is a high bar to meet, Mr. Rivera. You'll have a tough time proving that—

RIVERA: I don't think we'll have much trouble finding a judge who believes otherwise. As for your legal fees, Ms. Chen...

CHEN: My publisher would cover those.

RIVERA: If the work is deemed of a journalistic standard. We will probably spend a fair amount of time and money showing, of course, that it *isn't* that. Showing that your *relationship*— if that's the word—with a certain Leo Tresler compromised both your journalistic clarity and integrity.

LAWYER *(To Chen, quietly)*: Relationship?

Rivera goes on:

RIVERA: Let me ask you a question, Ms. Chen. How many copies do you think this could sell? I mean, if you hit it out of the park. Crazy numbers. *(Off Chen's silence)* What, fifty thousand? Right? The most you could expect? What would you make off that at sixteen ninety-five a book? With, what? A fifteen percent royalty? Not quite one hundred thirty thousand dollars? What if we paid you that? Right now. No. Let's say the book did twice that, no, ten times that? Five hundred thousand copies. Unheard of for a book like this. You'd net one point three million. Let's say for some reason they want to make a movie.... Highly unlikely, but let's say it happens. Another fifty thousand towards an option? Let's say it's a hit, you make another half-million in royalties.

Takes us up to around two million? Let's round it up to three. How about that? You take three million dollars, you go back to your publisher and say it's all unsubstantiated. It was a big mistake. You don't want to publish it anymore. Hand them back their tiny advance and go home a rich woman. Hmm? Why don't we save both our sides all the trouble ahead?

CHEN: Three million dollars.

LAWYER: That's a lot of money.

RIVERA: I'm going to leave you both to chew on that.

Rivera exits.

Pause.

—LIGHTS OUT ON CHEN AND HER LAWYER.

CHEN ADVANCES DOWNSTAGE.

—INTO A SPOTLIGHT.

AND STARES...

At the audience for a pregnant beat.

CHEN: I took the money—like everybody else did. Three million dollars. After taxes and legal fees, I ended up with one point four. I invested in a portfolio that included an array of high-yield junk bonds. I would double the money in ten years. Triple it ten years after that. At the close of the third quarter of 2017, I was worth nineteen million. I never wrote another word.

—LIGHTS OUT.

—LIGHTS UP ON:

LOW-SECURITY PRISON.

Yard. A picnic table.

Merkin and CURT, a prison guard. Merkin is making notes of some sort on a notepad.

Curt whistles quietly as he looks out the "window."

Checks his watch. Looks out the window again.

CURT: Sun setting a lot earlier now.

MERKIN: That's what happens.

CURT: But I mean a *lot* earlier. Days are already getting shorter. Then they roll the clocks back.

MERKIN: Rolled them forward. Have to roll them back. Daylight savings.

CURT: I never understood that. I mean—what are they saving?

MERKIN: I think the idea had something to do with candle wax.

CURT: What?

MERKIN: More light at the end of the day during summer meant less spent on candles I guess.

CURT: But we don't use candles anymore, Mr. Merkin.

MERKIN: I never liked it either.

Pause.

CURT: Well, I better be making the rounds. Make sure everyone's where they should be.

MERKIN *(Pushing a tin)*: You don't want another cookie?

CURT: Well, I mean, I won't say no. Those cookies from your friend. Amazing.

MERKIN: Yeah. Murray and I go way back. Listen, I'm almost done here. Just hold off a second. Before you go.

CURT: Okay.

Curt steps over to the table, takes a cookie from the tin.

MERKIN: So, looks to me like you'd be paying seven hundred dollars less in taxes if you *owned* your own place, Curt.

CURT: I keep telling you, with what money, Mr. Merkin?

MERKIN: You're making twenty-nine thousand here, right?

CURT: Yeah.

MERKIN: And your wife is bringing home another fifteen.

CURT: Yeah. Cleaning houses.

MERKIN: That's forty-four. Which means after taxes—

CURT: She's paid under the table.

MERKIN: Okay, that's even better. So that means, each month you guys have just over three thousand dollars.

CURT: Yeah.

MERKIN: You can reasonably afford a monthly payment at one-third of that. I mean you'd have to budget, but...

CURT: A thousand a month? That's...

MERKIN: Yes, that'll mean saving. But this way the saving is going into something that has value. Something that's yours. That will increase in value over time.

CURT: Kimmie's got the health issues, Mr. Merkin...

MERKIN: So your daughter's health expenses accounted for, that still leaves you seven hundred a month? Which means you can afford—about an eighty-thousand-dollar house.

CURT *(Surprised)*: Really?

MERKIN: All you'd need is eight thousand to put down.

CURT *(Picking up the pad, disbelieving)*: Eight thousand dollars?

MERKIN: You've gotta have that somewhere.

CURT: I don't. What comes in, goes right out. Like I said, the girl's not been good. *(Puts down the pad)* It's probably just as well, Mr. Merkin. I mean I look at those numbers there... it's like Chinese to me.

MERKIN: That's how they get you. It's how they get everyone. The system's speaking a different language, a language they know people don't understand. The second anyone tries to explain it, their eyes glaze over. That's by design. They make fools out of everyone. You know that old saying, a fool and his money are soon parted, right?

CURT: Yeah.

MERKIN: Well that's what it is. Make fools out of everyone, then take their money.

CURT: Is that what you were doing? Is that why you're here?

MERKIN: I suppose. The people I made fools out of, though, weren't folks like you, Curt. It was the people who were usually doing the fooling. I made fools out of the people in charge. They didn't like it.

Curt nods.

CURT: You're not, uh—I don't know. You're not like what they say about you.

MERKIN: Who is? *(Taking up the pad)* That's the problem with the system. It's always rigged against the little guy. I mean it shouldn't be so hard. The fact is, you have the income for a mortgage. You just don't have the down payment. There should be a way to make that work. *(Putting it together, working it out)* No money down. Sell the mortgage debt. Use the proceeds to secure insurance against default. Right. Right. Like junk. Now just sell it straight to the American people. Right.

Beat.

CURT: I'm gonna go do those rounds.

Curt exits.

Merkin goes to his table, energized, starts to make notes…

THE END

"NOTHING MAKES MONEY THE WAY MONEY MAKES MONEY"

A conversation between playwright Ayad Akhtar and director of new play development at La Jolla Playhouse Gabriel Greene

GG: *Junk* is the second of your plays that deals overtly with the world of finance. How did your fascination with the subject take root?

AA: My dad made a deal with me when I moved to New York in my early 20s. He's a ridiculously successful doctor, and I was still reading poetry. He was like, "We got to put some sense in this kid. Staring at paper all the time. Can we get him to stare at different paper?" So he said that if I read the *Wall Street Journal* every day, he'd pay my rent. For two years I read the *Wall Street Journal* every day—I was a dutiful son—and I started getting into economics. It was the beginning of a bull market, so money was everywhere: *The New Yorker* was writing about money, people were talking about money at book parties, everyone had their stock portfolio, and everybody was making money. I started to get into this stuff. I think my dad was hoping maybe I'd go into finance or something. I didn't, but that was my inculcation into the world of money, and that world has been an important part of my work.

That's the background context of writing this play. I've always wanted to write a play about finance. I feel like we don't understand how our lives are so completely dominated by finance. We don't get it. I didn't want to write a screed against finance; I wanted to write a thrilling story that was going to embed the audience in the *process* of capital—so that they could feel what it feels like, and why it's so compelling. And then at the end of the play they can make up their minds.

GG: And how has the play changed as it developed?

AA: I had an early draft of the play, which I think effectively embedded the audience in capital but didn't necessarily *enlist* them in the philosophical and social dimensions and consequences of what the process of capital is doing to our country. Over the last couple of years, Doug [Hughes] and I have been working toward a vision of how to enlist the audiences' sympathies in various ways, to make them experience the consequences of this thrilling buzz of making money that leaves us all impoverished in some spiritual way.

GG: In rehearsal today, we talked about the idea that wealth now connotes celebrity.

AA: It connotes more than that. It's ontology. Wealth is existential, wealth connotes *being*. One doesn't *exist* as a citizen in this advanced, late-capitalist moment without wealth. One has no *agency* without wealth. We exist in the grip of a corporate financial vise that squeezes everybody. I think that the aspect of wealth as a kind of measure of celebrity speaks to the way in which wealth is the only value that we still aspire to.

GG: There seems to be something almost Shakespearean—and I know you shy away from comparisons to Shakespeare....
AA: I mean, anybody should.

GG: But there is something Shakespearean about the way in which finance, power, and masculinity collide in what amounts to a modern-day "war play."
AA: Those are all interwoven thematic nubs that were at the heart of a global transformation that has been under way for a generation and a half, two generations. In the process, we're distracted by our chatter about identity politics and equality, distracted by these matters of our *individual* well-being. Our *collective* well-being has been undermined by this larger movement. I wanted to write about that process in a way that was human and engaging and that was thrilling. And it seemed to me that Shakespeare was somebody who was able to write about power and masculinity and succession in ways that were thrilling, so he became a kind of way of thinking about how to write this play. Yes, it's a silly thing to do—to try to write in dialogue with Shakespeare in that way—but there it is.

GG: When you and I first talked about *Junk,* you called it an origin myth for the economy that we've inherited.
AA: That's exactly right. I'm not really writing about that period; I'm writing about now. I'm using the mythos of that time to address matters of moment today. I do think that fundamental

philosophical debates around notions of shareholder rights, equity, and ownership are at the center of our democracy in a way that people don't understand. These are abstract things, but they go to the heart of our experience as citizens of this country, or as non-citizens, as it were.

I'm not trying to show anything about the economy; I'm trying to show a shift in the ethos, how we changed our feeling. We feel thoughts more than we think them, and I'm trying to show how the feeling/texture of the thought around money changed at a certain moment in our history. And we are very much in the consequences of that shift.

GG: A major component in that shift was junk bonds. They weren't new to the 1980s, but they became the means to accomplish a completely different, revolutionary end than what anybody had thought of before.

AA: The play is called *Junk* but it's not about junk bonds. The play is about the moment in American history when our relationship to debt changed. But it didn't even begin with junk bonds. It began with the Fed raising interest rates to twenty percent in the late seventies/early eighties, creating a climate where pursuing yields like that was even possible. The only way to get there was to turn debt into an asset, which is exactly what the treasury department did by letting interest rates run that high.

The real innovation of junk bonds in the era of the 1980s under [Michael] Milken was to create possibility. When you have cash, there is possibility. Junk became a means of vast capacity to raise a lot of cash. We see it today in the venture capital realm; if it weren't for corporate seed money, we wouldn't have the technological advances that we have. The precursor to that kind of disruptive financial support is junk bonds.

GG: And therein lies the central debate. There are those who extol the virtues of debt as a democratizing paradigm shift. It changes who gets a seat at the table—
AA: ... and who can own a house.

GG: And yet, very few would argue that when these bubbles inevitably burst, something went wrong.
AA: One of the problems of capitalism is that capital is expected to grow at a steady, constant, unabated rate. Capital is never subjected to the natural cycle of decay. Money in the bank is expected to grow, ideally at five percent, forever. Well, the reality is everything that grows goes through its seasons: spring, summer, fall, and winter. Capital has no fall and no winter; it is an eternal spring and summer. Which points to the extent to which capital is an abstraction. It must be returned to the cycle of decay because that is reality. The corrections are just part of the cycle of reality.

GG: Certain things have inherent value for survival: water, food, housing, clothes. When societies developed, currency emerged as a way to assign worth to that. Now, it feels like currency itself is of value.
AA: This is exactly right—this is the process of abstraction that I'm talking about. When you make things, when you exist within the real world of making and consuming, natural economic growth is at two percent. Capital—through investments—grows at five percent. At a certain point, when you have this process of

growth at two percent versus growth at five percent, the path diverges. Capital takes on a top-heavy quality; everything is transformed into a process of finance, usurped by this need for five percent. We no longer make cars to make cars, we make cars to create debts that yield five percent. We no longer sell food to sell food, we sell food because credit cards are used to buy the food, and that credit card debt yields five percent. Nothing makes money the way *money* makes money.

This is what's happened! We're arguing about what color our skin is, and in the process, the entire world has been sold out from under us. This is what's happened. I don't even know how you change it at this point, but the first step has got to be some understanding of what's really going on. The international mantra has become: Do less, make more. And within that context, the only role for labor is to be exploited. Labor can't compete; it's caught in the cycle of two percent.

GG: While everybody else is operating on four to five percent.

AA: Well, the few with ninety percent of the wealth, yes. And that gap continues to get wider and wider, and in the process has eroded any notion of collectivity. When a big-box store such as a Walmart moves into a community, eighty-six cents of every dollar spent there leaves the community. That puts pressure on local businesses, which, over time, only creates more dependency on the box stores, the chains. Which quickens the process of a community's impoverishment and the enrichment of those who have no stake in that community. That is the invisible centralization of power that exists at the heart of the corporate fiscal dictatorship. And I hesitate to use the word *dictatorship,* because it's going to make me sound like a commie. I'm not a communist. But the stakes are really high and education is the only thing that's going to make any difference.

GG: And what role can art play?

AA: To me, embedding the audience in the process of capital is not to moralize to them; they should make up their own minds about all of this stuff. But let's be fully *in it* emotionally, intellectually, physically, narratively. Let's be excited, let's be enthralled and absorbed by it so that we have some felt sense of what this is.

ACKNOWLEDGMENTS

So many contributed to the process resulting in this play. Thank you to:

André Bishop and Lincoln Center Theater, Chris Till and CAA, Marc Glick, Donna Bagdasarian, Amanda Watkins, Matthew Rego, Hank Unger, Mike Rego, Chris Ashley and La Jolla Playhouse, Oskar Eustis, Steve Klein, Emily Mann and the McCarter Theater, Johanna Pfaelzer and New York Stage and Film, Judy Clain, Nicole Dewey, Terry Adams and everyone at Little, Brown, Jim Nicola, Dave Caparelliotis and Lauren Port, P. Carl and David Dower, Kimberly Senior, Paige Evans, Indhu Rubasingham, Scott Rudin, Chuck Means, Jocelyn Clarke, J. T. Rogers, Greg Mosher, Michael Ritchie, Molly Smith, Mark Clements, Tony Taccone, Carole Rothman and Chris Birney, Alex Greenfield, Chris Campbell-Orrock, Phil Smith and Bob Wankel, Dasha Epstein, Sheldon Stone, Uwe Carstensen, Karin Beier.

I wrote the first draft of this play at Yaddo. I'm grateful to Elaina Richardson, Candace Waite, A. M. Homes and everyone in Saratoga for the gift of that time.

ABOUT THE AUTHOR

Ayad Akhtar is a playwright, a novelist, a screenwriter, and an actor. His novel, *American Dervish,* has been published in more than twenty languages. His plays have won numerous awards, including a Pulitzer Prize and OBIE Awards, and have been nominated for Tony and Olivier Awards. He is the recipient of an Award in Literature from the American Academy of Arts and Letters. He lives in New York City.